STRONTIUM DOG:
AMONG THE MISSING

THE ALPHA/STERNHAMMER YEARS #1

An Abaddon Books™ Publication
www.abaddonbooks.com
abaddon@rebellion.co.uk

First published in 2013 by Abaddon Books™, Rebellion Intellectual Property
Limited, Riverside House, Osney Mead, Oxford, OX2 0ES, UK.

10 9 8 7 6 5 4 3 2 1

Creative Director and CEO: Jason Kingsley
Chief Technical Officer: Chris Kingsley
Publishing Manager: Ben Smith
Editors: David Thomas Moore & Michael Rowley
Marketing and PR: Remy Njambi
Design: Sam Gretton, Oz Osborne & Maz Smith
Cover: Carlos Ezquerra

Strontium Dog created by
John Wagner, Alan Grant and Carlos Ezquerra.

ISBN (paperback): 978-1-78108-586-8

STRONTIUM DOG:
AMONG THE MISSING

THE ALPHA/STERNHAMMER YEARS #1

MATTHEW SMITH

ABADDON BOOKS

W W W . A B A D D O N B O O K S . C O M

Prologue

SHE KISSED HIM awake.

Fran leant across and brushed her lips against his, watching as consciousness surfaced in her husband's face, his eyes flickering behind the lids, his mouth forming a smile as he tasted her breath. Xander's sleep-encrusted lashes parted and he blearily studied her, his hand covering hers where it lay flat on his chest.

"Morning," he croaked, the last vestiges of his dreams dissipating.

"Morning."

He raised himself to respond more fully to her kiss, but even as he did so Fran could see his gaze straying to the clock on the bedside cabinet, and a sudden urgency stiffened him. He pecked her perfunctorily on the cheek, and swung his legs out from under the sheets.

"We've got plenty of time," she said, watching Xander pull on his voluminous dressing gown. "There's no need to panic."

"I know, I know. Just pre-flight anxiety, I suppose. I'll be all right once I'm on the shuttle."

"You're a worrier," she told him, matter-of-factly. "You think too much, that's your problem. Comes with having that big ol' brain of yours."

Xander laughed and shook his head, dragging down a suitcase from the top of the wardrobe and flipping it open on the bed.

"Anyway, you'll have Iris with you – she can hold your hand and keep you calm."

"That's true. Kid's unflappable." He started to throw underwear into the case, then stopped, looking back at her sitting up against the pillows, knees drawn together beneath her long T-shirt. "Are you sure you're going to be okay? It'll be the longest you two have been apart—"

Fran felt tears prick her eyes but willed them back. "It's only a month. It'll fly by, you'll see. I'll be out there to meet you both before you know it."

He nodded and resumed his packing. "I think she's the most excited about the trip out of any of us. Nothing fazes her, even a big move like this."

"Y'know, doc," Fran answered, rocking forward and padding towards him on all fours across the bedclothes, "our daughter probably isn't going to be awake for another thirty minutes, and bearing in mind these are our last hours together, why don't we make the most of it?"

He met her gaze – her eyebrow raised in mock-innocence – and without further persuasion pushed the suitcase onto the carpet.

THEY SHOWERED AND dressed, and once their daughter stirred and emerged on the landing, groggy with sleep, Xander and Fran beetled her to do the same. For all that her husband had acknowledged his nerves were unnecessary, Fran could still sense a fretfulness in his body language, a forced casualness in his tone. He wouldn't relax until they were in the air; more likely, when they had actually touched down on Hegley itself. It made the thought of their separation doubly difficult; unable to soothe or give comfort throughout the journey, she could only wave them off.

Fran went downstairs into the kitchen, and, flipping on the kettle, leant against the worktop, hugging herself against the morning chill. Her gaze settled on a stack of drawing pads that her daughter had left on the dining table the previous evening. Sketching was Iris's latest favourite pastime, and she'd discovered a talent that she certainly hadn't inherited from her mother and father. For her age, her imagination was formidable, and her skill at drafting fantastic figures and detailing the worlds in which they lived was extraordinary. Sheaves of paper were stacked on every free surface, and multi-coloured daubings were haphazardly stuck by magnets to the fridge-freezer.

It seemed their daughter was going to revolt against her scientist parents and embrace art. Where this creative leaning had come from, Fran didn't know, but she felt no disappointment at the thought of her child taking a different path from her mum and dad. Quite the opposite; conscious of the long hours of research that she'd had to endure, the academic trawl to attain her current position, and working days spent squinting at data on a computer screen, Fran relished the thought of Iris being free from that. She was the spark of life that reminded her and Xander of what lay outside the lab: this chaotic bundle of energy and infectious enthusiasm that couldn't be quantified, predicted or analysed.

The kettle squealed, and as she splashed hot water into a pair of mugs she realised just how quiet it was going to be without the two of them, how big the house would seem, and how lonely she would feel. She would be making tea for only herself from tomorrow. Reaching into the fridge for the milk, she caught sight of the girl's yoghurts and bottles of juice, which would go unconsumed. They would all have to be thrown out, but for the moment she just closed the fridge door. She wanted to keep her family close, if only in small reminders, for as long as she could.

Xander appeared in the hallway and placed a suitcase beside the front door. He accepted the tea that she passed him with a smile.

"You want anything to eat?" she asked.

He grimaced. "Not very hungry."

"You'll feel worse on an empty stomach."

He raised his eyebrows over the rim of the mug. "I can't imagine how."

"At least some toast," she persisted. "You don't want to feel sick on top of everything else."

He nodded, conciliatory. He turned the mug in his hands, his mind elsewhere. He glanced at his watch, crossed the kitchen and turned on the flatscreen TV embedded in the wall, tuning it to a news channel. The reporter was standing outside the mutant ghetto in

Dartford while the military swarmed around him, flames dancing in the background. There'd been more violent disturbances overnight and the government was locking it down. Statistics scrolled across the bottom: many, many dead.

"Are you sure you want to hear this now?" Fran asked.

Xander waved the words away as if the question was immaterial, the gesture far too blasé to fool her. "I wanted to catch the travel report, check there aren't any problems on the roads."

She turned away to finish preparing Iris's breakfast, staring down at the small bowl in front of her, the heaped cereal and the little spoon abutting from it, and felt a sharp pang of guilt for the world into which they'd brought their daughter, a planet they were supposed to be trying to change for the better. She and Xander, in their work for Galactic Health Organisation, were part of a department charged with sourcing solutions for the high infant mortality rate on Earth since the Atom War. Background radiation, contaminated water and food supplies and substandard living conditions had left children dying at a rate similar to that of the nineteenth century. The problem was far worse amongst the muties in the shanty towns, of course, but the politicians were less concerned about them than they were the nice normal families that represented the majority of their voters.

Fran shouted up the stairs for Iris to hurry. The girl had been desperate to come with them; similar trips had been no more than a few days at most, but the imminent medical summit on Hegley could stretch to a couple of months. They couldn't turn her down. As it happened, research deadlines and an unavoidable presentation meant that Fran couldn't join her husband and daughter until several weeks later, so the two of them would be flying ahead.

Iris came lolloping down the stairs, a mess of straw-blonde hair poking out from beneath a pink cap. She picked up her cereal bowl from the worktop and carried it carefully over to the table, seating herself and spooning heaps of wheat flakes into her mouth.

"Where's your bag?" Fran asked.

"I left it in my room," she mumbled as she chewed. "You were calling for me to come downstairs."

"Couldn't you have brought it down with you?"

"I haven't finished packing."

"We can't hang about, honey," Xander said, clicking the TV off. "We'll have to make a move shortly."

"I'm nearly done," she protested, scraping her spoon around the bottom of the bowl.

"If you'd made a start on it last night…" Fran started, wincing inside at her words. She sounded like her own mother. The look that Iris shot her felt well deserved, and she finished her breakfast in silence.

"C'mon, we've got to motor," Xander reiterated, taking the empty bowl from his daughter and directing her back towards her bedroom with two hands on her little shoulders. She swigged her orange juice in one gulp and passed the glass to her mother without a word as she went by. "Clean your teeth and finish your packing. I want you back down here in fifteen minutes. Scoot." He raised his eyebrows in amused tolerance at his wife as the girl scrambled up the stairs.

"Can you clear up down here?" Fran asked. "I want to chivvy her along."

"Sure. I'll start loading the car." He glanced again at his watch. "Remind her: fifteen minutes, or I'm leaving without her."

Fran followed the sounds of her daughter as Iris clattered from the bathroom into her bedroom, taps dripping in her wake. Fran picked up a stray towel lying damp on the tiles and hung it over the radiator, then rapped once on Iris's half-open door before entering. The six-year-old was kneeling in the centre of her room, an over-stuffed suitcase before her, its shell festooned with stickers of cartoon characters.

"You're never going to shut that, let alone carry it," Fran remarked, perching on the edge of her unmade bed.

"I can't decide what to take and what to leave behind," Iris said, sifting through a selection of T-shirts. A tangle of stuffed toys lay heaped at her right hand, a drawing pad and her pencil case beside them.

"You can't take it all," Fran answered, getting onto her knees so that she was level with the girl. "You've got to leave something behind. It'll all be here when you get back, don't worry. And anything you find you need we can buy out there." She removed a bundle of clothes from the suitcase, cast an eye over them, and placed them on the bed. "See, now you don't need any of that."

"Can't I put it into another bag?"

"You can only take one onto the shuttle, honey. It's the rules."

"Well, what about Artie?" She held up a brown monkey from the collection of toys, its limbs hanging loose from her hand. "If I take him, I won't have room for Gary." She dangled a small fluffy kitten under her mother's nose, its black-bead eyes staring lifelessly at her.

"Then you'll have to make a choice," Fran said sternly, continuing to sort through Iris's superfluous wardrobe. She'd managed to halve the contents of the suitcase, to the point where it looked like it could be zippered shut.

"But I *can't...*"

"Iris, it's either one or neither. Make a decision. We don't have time to dither."

The girl glanced at each of the animals in turn then grumpily threw the monkey amongst the clothes. Fran scooped up the drawing materials, slid them into a side pocket, and closed the case, the zipper struggling but holding firm. "There," she said, getting to her feet and grasping its handle to test its weight; it was manageable. "We got there in the end."

Iris didn't reply, and Fran stroked her cheek. "Sorry, love, but that's what travelling's like. You have to make do with the basics. Decide what's important, and leave anything else behind. Like I said, it'll all be here waiting for you when you get back. Okay?"

The girl nodded. Fran crouched beside her once again. "You're sure you still want to come? It's a long journey. If you're having second thoughts, tell me."

"No, I want to go," Iris said quickly, real excitement behind the words. "It's just... it'll be such a long time till I'm home again, that's all." She glanced around the bedroom. "I feel a bit sad that I'm going to be away from... everything."

Fran hugged her, pressing her cheek against her daughter's hair. "I know," she whispered into Iris's ear, feeling the girl's hands clutch at her midriff in a tight embrace. "It'll be okay." They relinquished their hold on each other, eyes moist, and Fran straightened Iris's baseball cap, which she'd knocked askew, then picked up the suitcase. "C'mon, let's get downstairs before your dad starts beeping the hooter. You ready?"

"I'm ready."

FRAN STOOD IN the porch, arms folded, watching as Xander loaded the last of the bags into the car and slammed the boot shut. He turned to look back at her, and tears pricked her eyes again; she wiped them away with the heel of her hand. Iris, standing beside him, ran and embraced her mother's legs. Fran crouched and hugged her daughter to her for long moments, feeling her rapid heartbeat against her chest.

"I'll give you a vid-call once we land," Xander said, putting an arm around Iris's shoulders, pulling her close. The girl was downcast, sniffing.

Fran nodded, her voice catching in her throat. "See you soon." She clutched the lapel of his jacket and gently pulled him forward, kissing him tenderly, before releasing him. He smiled and guided a sullen Iris towards the car, strapping her into the back seat.

The last Fran saw of them was the back of their heads through the rear windscreen, an acknowledging wave from Xander as they pulled out onto the road, and then they were gone.

Sixteen hours later, not long after she'd heard about the explosion, there was a knock at Fran's door.

Chapter One

It was an old maxim, but that didn't make it any less true: just because they're not smart doesn't mean they're not dangerous. Quite the opposite, in fact; crims with brains you could anticipate their next move, work their motive. The idiots, on the other hand, would try anything, risking their own lives as much as those around them. Dolts were a law unto themselves, and as a consequence lethal.

Johnny found himself musing on this observation as the wall of the stables he was sheltered behind was shredded by gunfire, woodchips spinning off in all directions with each ballistic punch. He shook off a tiny spar that landed on his arm and redoubled his grip on his blaster; yeah, these weren't rocket scientists, that much was clear, and they weren't going to take the sensible option and hand themselves in quietly. No, that would require some degree of forethought, a realisation of what they were up against and the inevitable outcome. Dunderheads let loose indiscriminately with plasma rifles because that was their default setting, the other alternatives never occurring to them.

What the hell. Warrant said *dead or alive*. The universe wasn't going to lose much sleep over the passing of these five evolutionary specimens.

At least, he presumed there were still five. He'd lost sight of Wulf, and guessed he was still round back of the courthouse where he'd been pinned down; he could very well have already dealt with one or two. Johnny hadn't heard any commotion to that effect, but even though he wasn't duly concerned – the big guy could take care of himself well enough, as he'd demonstrated on several occasions – better to err on the side of caution and take it as read that the Crawdad Brothers were, as a unit and as of this moment, intact.

He needed to get a better idea of where they were firing on him from, and so he edged back to take a look, his eyes piercing the stables themselves and focusing on the adjoining building. The grey outline of a figure was visible leaning around an open side doorway, raking the immediate vicinity with his weapon. There had to be one on the roof too, judging by the angle of attack; he craned his head and caught a glimpse of a silhouetted shape bobbing behind the parapet. Turning his attention to what was in front of him, Johnny realised that there were still morks alive in the stables: they whinnied and stamped their feet as they pressed themselves against the wall, furthest away from the plasma blasts, which had ignited the wood and straw. Smoke was starting to bloom. A handful of the animals lay dead on the floor, scorched and seared where they'd taken bolts intended for him.

Johnny felt bad for using them as cover, but the structure had been the nearest solid object between him and a super-heated barrel pointed in his direction. No need for them to suffer any longer, he reasoned. He blew out the wall that was already aflame with a single shot, leaping through the resultant ragged hole. Arm over his mouth, his lungs already tightening, he hurried towards the panicking creatures and kicked free the restraining bar that was preventing their escape, yanking off a set of reins hanging from a nearby hook as he did so. The morks thundered half-crazed towards freedom; Johnny messily looped the reins around the body of one of them as it passed him and clung on, legs wrapped around its rump. He could feel its muscles rolling beneath him, its hide slick with sweat. His mount blundered into the fresh air, the S/D agent dangling precariously from its side, one hand clutching the straps, the other attempting to bring his Westinghouse to bear.

There'd been half a dozen of the animals that had emerged from the stables, and the sudden stampede clearly disorientated his opponent, who began to fire even more wildly than before, unsure of his target. A couple of morks went down, heads disintegrated. But the distraction was enough: Johnny pulled himself over the back of his ride as it galloped into the open space between the two buildings and took his shot, snapping out the left kneecap of the Crawdad gunman in the doorway. It wasn't ideal – moving at speed and half attached to a mork had thrown his aim somewhat – but it had put the guy out of action momentarily; he collapsed onto his backside, dropping the gun and shrieking. Johnny leapt and rolled, scooting away from the paths of the careering creatures, and jogged towards the prone figure, a few bolts from the pinhead on the roof kicking up dust behind him.

He didn't have time to mess around – when he saw Leeroy Crawdad (Johnny recognised him as one of the younger siblings, an unmistakable rainbow-coloured ridge across his reptilian head that the whole family sported) had realised he was approaching and was reaching for his rifle, dragging himself towards it, his busted leg leaving a thin trail of blood, Alpha put a slug through his heart without breaking a step. He hopped over the body and crossed the threshold.

It was cooler inside, a shady relief from the unrelenting glare of the Costallarian sun, all bare tiles and sandstone mosaics on the walls. It was a pretty basic courthouse, but then Kardun, the major landmass on Costallarus, was pretty basic all over, a backwater civilisation largely untouched by galactic progress unless wanted crims fetched up here, looking for a bolthole, and brought with them the kind of high-tech bad news that on-the-lam felons tended to accumulate. Local law enforcement often struggled to cope, more used to running down grain thieves or locking up drunks till they dried out. You could see why villains found planets like this so attractive; even the dumbest, with enough firepower, could intimidate the natives, and should a police officer happen to get lucky, the jails didn't even approach maximum security. When Johnny and Wulf had tracked down and taken custody of two of the Crawdad Brothers, Nimbus and Dofar, here on Kardun, standard – not to mention politically circumspect – operating procedure was to present them to the authorities: their world, their prisoners to do with as they wished. The S/D agents would get paid back at the Doghouse, so what happened to their charges once they handed them over was not usually their concern. Johnny would often feel uneasy at this end of the business, but it was something to become accustomed to as you learnt the way the universe operated; Wulf, he was surprised to discover, took it very much in his stride, the Viking shrugging his shoulders and accepting that the jurisdiction should determine the punishment. He was quite puritanical like that – his culture had its own manners and code of ethics, and if one transgressed them then you had to face the music of the society you had aggrieved.

Trouble was, the Kardun court officials were painfully undermanned and outgunned when the three remaining Crawdads came calling to spring their siblings and tore the front off the building in the process. Less intellectually challenged lowlifes would've possibly considered waiting until after the heavily armed bounty hunters had left the vicinity before launching a rescue bid, but that was the Brothers for you. The fact was that they'd left a string of murders, robbed banks and stolen vehicles in their wake, with little disguise as to who were the perpetrators, and the rewards for their capture or execution were racking up across the system; Johnny and Wulf had caught the scent of two of the gang, but the entire family suddenly crashing in was kind of a windfall for them. There were creds to be had, provided the S/D agents could stay alive for the next three minutes.

Alpha picked his way carefully over the corpses of the Costallari, guards who chiefly hadn't stood a chance against such single-minded brutality. He could hear the rattle and fizz of energy-weapon exchange from ahead, and surmised that it was his partner keeping them busy. The Strontium Dog rounded a corner into the main chamber and saw two of the crims pouring fire through an open section of the rear wall where it had collapsed. Johnny pondered for a second: this was a smash and grab, so the only reason the Crawdads were still here had to be that one of the clan was being prevented from fleeing. Also, they had to have a means of escape, which was presumably what the member on the roof was up to. Alpha decided to cut off that line of retreat while he had the chance. He retraced his steps to the corridor, found the stairs and bounded up them two at a time until they ended at the maintenance door. There wasn't much value in subtlety at this point in the game; he aimed the Westinghouse and took the door off its hinges with a Number 4 Cartridge. He dived through the smoke, his eyes helping to pick out the silhouette of the startled and coughing Crawdad brother – Jeremiah – swinging his rifle back and forth, and shot him in the neck. He slumped down dead onto the sun-warmed stone next to the open-top hover-skoomer that was their getaway craft. Its engine rumbled as it idled. Just to make doubly sure that no one was going anywhere, Johnny popped its hood and tore out a few ignition wires.

He crouch-ran to the rear of the building and peered over the parapet into a courtyard: he could see Wulf hunkered behind a row of jubjub trees, plasma beams scorching the shrubbery around him. The reason for the Crawdads' delay was plain: Nimbus lay prone a few feet from where the Viking was sheltering, wounds in his stomach and shoulder. His brothers couldn't get close enough to drag him free without entering Wulf's line of fire. Still, they weren't giving up. The reptilians were, Johnny mused, surprisingly loyal for cold-hearted killers.

"Wulf!" Alpha yelled. The big guy looked around and caught sight of him, raising his hand in acknowledgement. His face and beard were smeared with soot. Johnny pointed down to the two Crawdads somewhere below and unhooked a shrap grenade from his bandolier, nodding to it. Wulf nodded back and disappeared behind the foliage. Alpha leant over the edge of the roof and dropped the explosive as close as possible to the open section of wall, then twisted away and fell to his knees.

The flash-boom seemed to rock the courthouse itself, an ear-splitting crack that momentarily sucked the noise out of the world. As the senses returned, so the screams began to peal, Johnny taking them as his cue to finish this. He ran down to the ground floor and found what was left of Dofar and Cokely Crawdad spread up the walls, their miniscule animal brains refusing to accept that they weren't still alive. Their limbs were in four different corners of the room and their detached heads, wedged halfway to the ceiling, looked like trophies brought home from the Neverglades. They wailed and frothed until Alpha shot them both silent. Wulf emerged from his hiding place to join him, Happy Stick propped against his shoulder.

"By gott, Johnny," he murmured, rubbing his brow with one hand. "Not good for der hangover."

"Not much good for anyone," Alpha replied, surveying the damage, his own head feeling like it was ringing. He glanced towards Nimbus. "The last one still alive?"

"I doubt it, but vill check." Wulf walked back and poked the body with his hammer; it didn't stir. "No, cold as der cucumber. Must've been finished off by der explosion."

"Ah, well. Recorder will have got it all." Johnny tapped the side of his helmet where the tiny camera was housed, making an ache blossom in his temple. He winced. A warm bunk in an outgoing shuttle was looking increasingly inviting. "C'mon, let's go."

"We leave quite der mess behind," Wulf remarked, as they strode away, flames flickering from the burning stables.

"Not a clean business, my friend. Not a clean business."

OF ALL THE elements Johnny had asked Wulf to accept when it came to living in the twenty-third century, the Doghouse had remained perhaps the hardest to swallow. That wasn't to say that any of it – the star travel, the weaponry, the alien races and languages – had been especially easy for a Viking from 793AD to suddenly find himself immersed in, but Alpha got the impression that Wulf believed himself on a warrior's journey at the whim of the gods, passing through the veil from the world he knew to somewhere unutterably different. It had required a phenomenal strength of will, Johnny thought, for his mind not to just snap at the extreme culture shock, but the big guy was made of sterner stuff; quietly, stoically unfazed by his surroundings, steadfast and determined to stand beside 'Johnny Veird-Eyes', to whom he believed he owed a life-debt after the Ragnarok case. The way he'd adapted was a marvel. On the few occasions when Alpha had tried to talk to him about it – answer any questions he might have, address concerns – anxious that Wulf may be storing up the loneliness and the uncomprehending insanity of his situation until one day he blew an irretrievable fuse, the Viking had smiled and replied that he needed no counsel. The tacit implication was that this was what it was, and to peer too deeply into how he felt about it would ruin a little of the magic, affront Destiny that had laid this path before him by querying its motives. His fondness for drink probably helped as well.

But the Doghouse... Alpha had to admit the Doghouse had freaked Wulf right out.

It had been just under a year since the time-job and his new partner had returned with him to the Search/Destroy headquarters. Beside Harvey, the base's garrulous liaison with the Galactic Crime Commission, and a few admin staff, Wulf was a rare norm among the Stronts – even rarer (in fact unheard of) was a non-mutant becoming an S/D agent. He was viewed with outright suspicion and hostility by Johnny's peers; many treated him, it had to be said, no better than they'd been treated by the norm majority back on Earth. Apart from the most bloodthirsty, few mutants would admit that bounty hunting would be their chosen profession if any other avenues were open to them, and yet in the face of Wulf joining the brethren they became abruptly proprietorial, claiming it improper that a norm could come in and be an agent. If this was all mutants were allowed to do, then it should solely be the preserve of mutants. Stronts got heated over the issue, as Stronts have a tendency to do when their livelihood is threatened, and Alpha had to go in to bat for his friend more than once, pointing out the unedifying spectacle of raw prejudice as he broke a couple of noses.

From Wulf's perspective, all he saw were strange, misshapen half-humans berating his presence, and judging by the look in his eyes it seemed he regarded them as either an ongoing hallucination or demons populating a hellish dimension into which he'd willingly been thrust. Either way, he'd kept tightening his grip on his warhammer, a hair's breadth away from launching himself at the monsters, yet was calmed by Johnny, drawing his attention to his white, pupil-less eyes and remarking that he was no different from the others on the station. It was just varying degrees of mutation. His alpha rays enabled him to take a peek inside the Viking's head and he gleaned, unsurprisingly, a sneckload of confusion and frustration, which he did his best to counter by explaining that nobody here was his enemy, and that they were all his equal.

Within a week, Wulf had won them over, his propensity for alcohol making him a favourite in the bar and his stout heart proving irresistible to dislike. Few could dispute his loyalty, and the fact that he was watching the back of John Alpha – a man who'd done plenty for the cause of mutantkind, and knew which side of the line he stood – made them admit that the big bearded Viking was actually a stand-up guy (when, of course, he could stand up, and wasn't drunkenly snoozing under a table somewhere). Harvey, meanwhile, saw no problem with Wulf becoming an S/D agent – the Stronts were all scum in his opinion, and if the Scandinavian oaf wanted to partner with one of the freaks then good luck to him.

Watching the Doghouse grow closer from his porthole window, Johnny could scarcely believe it had been eleven months since he'd first introduced the barely comprehending Wulf to his rancorous comrades. If he was honest, it had gone better than he had anticipated; not just easing a norm into the mutants' ranks, but also their work together. Johnny was, since childhood, a natural loner, most comfortable in his own company; his family situation and his mutation had necessitated it from the start, but it carried over into his adult life too; he found himself preferring to be a man apart. No one, as far as he was aware, took this as aloofness, but rather it was simply acknowledged he operated most efficiently solo. But Wulf had changed that: not only was he a fearsome, capable fighter, but he could also penetrate the fug of maudlin introspection that Alpha was prone to, bring him out of himself. The Viking's joys were straightforward enough – beer, women, the acquisition of money, and a ruck if the mood took him – and he saw little value in brooding. To that end, he was Johnny's perfect foil, drawing him from dark thoughts with a live-for-the-moment philosophy; just as he was intolerant of loudmouths and petty buffoons, so too did he refuse to countenance too much self-indulgence. Alpha had to admit, it was what he needed; if he ever became locked in some mordant obsession, his ruminations could be dispelled with a word from Wulf, a well-judged wake-up call that managed to be delivered brusquely but with a degree of sensitivity. They were a good team.

Disembarking, Johnny relished the wash of familiarity on returning to the S/D headquarters; it was pretty much the nearest thing to home now that Earth was a no-go zone. He wasn't planning on spending the rest of his days living out of it – he envisioned using the creds he was saving to buy a plot of land on some quiet planet somewhere, far from the bloodshed and hatred that had scarred much of his life up to now – but for the time being it was good to have an anchor, a fixed point to return to. He felt a strong bond with those of his kind: they were people he had served with during the war, or who had relatives that had died by his side. Collectively, they'd been through a great deal together. He nodded at the Stronts he passed as he and Wulf made their way to the processing section to claim the bounty on the Crawdads.

It was while he was handing over the recording device for the clerk to verify that Harvey stuck his head around the door. "Alpha? You got a visitor. Been waiting for you for the best part of five hours."

"Visitor?"

Harvey shrugged. "A doctor, she said she was. From Earth. Asked for you by name, refused to talk to anyone else. Fran something, I think. You expecting her?"

Johnny glanced at Wulf and shook his head. "News to me."

"Well, she sure knew who you were. Seemed a bit of an oddball, if you ask me. I put her in the accommodation suite to keep her out of the way." Harvey slapped the door as he disappeared behind it back into his own office. "See what she wants and get rid of her, eh? Last thing I need is some weirdo mutie-chaser causing trouble."

Chapter Two

She was sitting with her back to them when they entered, gazing out the window at the stars beyond. The accommodation suite was the public face of the Doghouse, a smart, comfortable lounge where the non-criminal, non-Stront elements were directed to upon arriving: guests, relatives, visiting dignitaries. If they didn't stray between it and the shuttle docking bays, then they didn't get to see the HQ's ugly underbelly: the holding cells, the vomit-flecked bars, the weapons racks. Here, the bounty-hunting business looked almost presentable. The woman was perched on the edge of one of the sofas, hands on her lap, back straight, and even from a distance Johnny could see there wasn't a trace of ease in her pose; she was tense, fretful, possibly afraid.

He and Wulf were halfway across the room and about to speak when she turned and stood, perhaps having seen their reflections in the glass. Dressed in a sober trouser suit, she was dark and attractive, mid-thirties, shoulder-length auburn hair, brown eyes ringed with redness where she'd been either crying or rubbing them, or both. She nodded at them hesitantly, then extended her hand, which the mutant shook firmly.

"John Alpha, I presume," she said, her voice catching a little. The educated background behind her Home Counties accent was unmistakable.

"That's me." He jabbed a thumb over his shoulder. "This is Wulf Sternhammer, my partner."

Her eyebrows raised slightly as she appraised the other man, and smiled tightly. "Oh... I was under the impression you worked alone."

"I did, until recently," Johnny answered. "Wulf's not long been an agent." He chose not to elaborate, conscious of the fact that he didn't want to make the Viking sound like a souvenir he'd picked up on his travels.

"Oh," she repeated.

"Is a problem?" Wulf rumbled.

"No, not at all," she said quickly, gathering herself. "I'm sorry, my head's not really together, and, to be honest, I was a bit nervous about coming here. I've not ever dealt with..."

"...mutants?" Alpha asked.

"No, no, Search/Destroy personnel. No, I've worked with... with your people extensively, as part of my research." She sucked in a breath, rolled her eyes. "Listen to me – I haven't even introduced myself. I'm Doctor Frances Persimmion; I'm a genetic scientist based out of Livingstone University in New London, but I also work for the government. For the past few years they've had me looking at birth defects and infant mortality since the war." She paused and met his gaze; or was maybe studying his empty eyes, he couldn't tell. "You probably know first-hand the damage the fallout has wrought."

"Pretty much all of us here are victims of the war, doctor. That, and everything that came after." He folded his arms. "What can we help you with? I was told you'd asked to see me personally."

"Yes," she said. She reached behind her, grabbed a briefcase from the sofa and placed it on a nearby table. Her hand was trembling, Alpha noted. "Yes, as I said, I was unsure about employing your services, but I'm becoming desperate. Sorry, that sounds bad. You know what I mean. I've exhausted all other avenues... and I didn't know what else to do." Her breathing was growing harsher as she fumbled at the lock on the case, her eyes moistening. Johnny laid a hand on her arm.

"Doctor," he said, gently guiding her into a chair. "Sit down, take your time, and tell us what's going on."

She squeezed her eyes shut, hung her head, and emitted a single, sharp sob, then brought a hand to her mouth as if she hadn't meant for it to escape. She sat like that for a few moments, a tear trickling down her cheek, before she opened her eyes, sniffed, wiped away the moisture from her face, and clicked free the case's catch. She retrieved a datapad, swiped her finger across it, glanced at the screen and handed it to Alpha. "Did you hear about what happened on Hegley, to Flight 307?" she asked, clearing her throat.

Johnny shook his head. "Me and Wulf have been outside the system for the past month." He looked down at the device she'd passed to him: it was a newsfeed, broadcasting from the scene of an apparent disaster. He skim-read the salient details – shuttle exploded upon approach to landing, everyone on board killed, terrorist bomb suspected – and checked the date. This had happened over a couple of weeks ago. "Where is Hegley's Moon, anyway?"

"Banaris Quadrant," the doctor replied. "It's a small colony with an indigenous population, but it's traditionally where the Galactic Health Organisation holds its annual summits. Well, obviously, that's been cancelled now, after what happened."

"Okay." Alpha passed the datapad to Wulf. "And where do you fit into this?"

She swallowed, her right hand unconsciously fiddling with a pendant around her neck, and her gaze strayed once more to the window. "My... my husband and daughter were on that flight. He's a genetic scientist too; he was heading out there to attend the meeting. Iris, my little girl, she went with him. I was going to follow later; I had some work that needed finishing."

"I'm sorry."

Tears welled again, and she was now gripping the pendant in a fist. "I got the call hours later. At first they thought the ship had crashed, but it was later determined that it had exploded a couple of minutes before touchdown. They found thermite traces amongst the wreckage – there'd been a bomb on board." Johnny could see the muscles in her jaw pulsing as she struggled to remain composed. "Nobody had had a chance, the craft was completely destroyed. The authorities sifted through the bodies and checked them off against the manifest: Iris... was among them."

Alpha could sense the rawness of the woman's grief, her whole body imperceptibly shaking as if there was something inside she wanted to release. "And your husband...?"

She gave one brief jerk of the head. "Missing."

"Missing?"

"They couldn't find him; he wasn't among the dead. Everyone else on the shuttle – passengers, crew, cabin staff – had all been accounted for, their remains recovered. But Xander... Xander had vanished."

"He was definitely on board?"

The woman nodded. "No question. Boarding pass has him registered as passing through the gate, as does security footage. There were no discrepancies with the passenger list upon take-off."

"Vot do der authorities say?" Wulf chimed in.

"They're giving the impression that they know just as much as me. But I was visited by a representative of the spaceline as well as a colony officer from Hegley and a member of the Counter Terrorist Unit several days after the explosion, once Xander became an anomaly. They quizzed me about his movements, why he was on the shuttle, his research. Bottom line is, the fact that they can't find him has made him the number one suspect for the bombing. By all accounts, Hegley police are conducting a massive manhunt, combing the moon for him."

"No other suspects?" Johnny enquired.

"That indigenous population I mentioned – the Banabloos. Things are tense between them and the colonists, something to do with recognition of their religion, but they've never done anything on this scale before. Even so, the humans are cracking down on their townships, just in case. The brother-in-law of Hegley's mayor was among the dead, so that's stoked everything to boiling point."

The mutant ran a hand over his chin. "This is going to sound like a stupid question, but I have to ask – there's no way in your mind that your husband could be responsible?"

He'd expected her to vehemently deny such an accusation; instead, she looked weary, as if she'd not only expected it, but had also already answered it many times before. "No, not a chance. Xander is not a murderer. He would not kill our daughter. And there has been nothing to gain from this act – nothing has been achieved."

"Except der deaths of a few hundred colonists," Wulf said, glancing at Johnny, who nodded in reply. "It serves der natives very well."

"Brings the media focus onto them," Alpha mused. "Shines a light on the situation on Hegley, which would otherwise have gone unreported." He turned his attention back to Fran. "You believe he's still alive, don't you?"

"Yes, he has to be. I can think of no other explanation for why his body was not found. Somehow, he was thrown clear, and landed far from the crash. But the shock gave him amnesia, maybe, disoriented him to such an extent that he couldn't talk to anyone, didn't know where he was or what had happened. He could've been wandering for days, unaware of his own name, lost, confused."

"But the police haven't found him yet."

"If they do, it scares me to imagine what he may suffer at their hands. They're out for blood; they'll want to see the perpetrator pay. Already the rumours are spreading that Xander is in league with the Banabloos. He may be alive, but he's not safe." She dropped her head, her voice not much more than a murmur. "The longer he's out there, the more I can feel myself going insane. I need to know where he is, I need to find him, before he's made a scapegoat. That's why I came to you."

Alpha was silent for a moment. "Why me, particularly?"

She shrugged, not meeting his gaze. "I did some research. I was getting nothing out of Hegley's police – as far as they were concerned, Xander was guilty, and they wouldn't listen to anything I had to say. No one on Earth would take my case; they said it was out of their jurisdiction. I tried talking to some private investigators to see if they would help me track him down, but they all refused to go near Hegley, claiming it was about to explode if relations between the colonists and the natives deteriorated any further. I think one of them might have said something about me needing a Strontium Dog at my side if I was going to get in and out of there alive." She finally looked up, face hard and pale. "I read about your role in the mutant uprising, Mr Alpha: how you were instrumental in the defeat of the Kreelers, how your people owe you a lot—"

"No one owes me anything. And plenty would agree with me that I didn't change enough."

"Nevertheless, you seemed an honourable, decent man – one who recognised injustice, and was prepared to help others. I hoped I could hire you to track Xander down for me before it's too late. Of course, I'll pay you whatever I can afford."

Johnny appeared to consider this for a second, then stepped away from the table. His back to the woman, he said, "Keep your money, Dr Persimmion. I'm afraid we can't take the job."

Wulf glanced sharply at his partner, but said nothing. Fran blinked, surprised, and stood from her chair. "Please... name your fee, and it's yours."

"It's not as simple as that. This is an ongoing investigation for the local law-enforcement agencies. I'm sympathetic to your loss, and I'm sorry I can't do more to help, but if bounty hunters were to suddenly step into the middle of a situation like Hegley, we'd be arrested within an hour of arriving. The Galactic Crime Commission would have no sway there – we'd be unlicensed operatives."

Fran visibly sagged. "What can I do?"

"Get your lawyer working on extradition papers. If your husband is found alive, then they'll ensure he's treated respectfully and within the terms of the galactic convention. Hegley will fight them, but if it's a colony, it will be bound by accordance with Earth. That's all I can suggest."

She nodded and quickly gathered her things, her face flushed and downcast. "Thank you for your time, anyway, and for your honesty, Mr Alpha. Now, I have to get home; my daughter's remains are being shipped back for burial."

"I'm sorry," Johnny repeated as she swept past out of the suite, then caught Wulf glaring at him. "What?"

"Der woman has just lost her child, and is trying to find her husband. Surely ve can help her?"

"It's a matter for the cops on the ground. We start poking our noses in, we're going to stir up a whole heap of trouble."

"It vouldn't be der first time ve've gone in under der radar. Vot about der Groodus snatch? That vas a private contract. You've never objected before about going in vhere ve might not be vanted."

"It's still a big risk. Anyway, I thought you were all about respecting the way other planets did things."

"This isn't custom and practise, this is a witch-hunt with little evidence to back it up. And risk? *Pah!*" Wulf slammed his hammer down on the table. "It's about saving an innocent man's life. And you agree he *is* innocent."

Johnny conceded the point. "I took a peek in her head – she believes he is, at any rate."

"Ve vould let them string him up rather than put ourselves in der firing line? That does not sound honourable to me. And you know they are using him as an excuse to bully der natives."

"Oh, yeah, the norms are acting true to form. But it's not up to us to fight every battle—"

"That is vot this is *really* about," Wulf snapped. "It's because she's from Earth. You vould refuse to help because of who she is, vot she represents."

"She's part of the government, she said so herself," Alpha replied sullenly. There was no little truth in his words. "They've been the first to treat us like dirt."

"She's a voman asking for our assistance, and desperate enough to pay for it. You think because ve turn her down that she's going to stop there? She came to you because she thought she could trust you – now, she's going to hire one of those cold-blooded voorms out there, who von't hesitate in exploiting her. She'll be a sheep amongst der wolves. Once they smell der creds, trying to find her husband vill be der last thing on their minds."

Damn it, Alpha thought, for a Viking warrior he was pretty bloody astute. The fact was, his reluctance to accept the case did stem from a dislike of doing norms' work; his past experience and treatment at their hands had made him jaded. Although one could argue that being a Search/Destroy agent and by extension an employee of the GCC was toiling under the yoke of the same authorities that had marginalised mutants the galaxy over, he preferred to see a Stront's job as bringing to book those that threaten and intimidate others, ensuring that the innocent didn't have to suffer the persecution his kind had. He was calling to account the bad men and women that the warrants threw his way more for his own personal desire to witness the guilty punished than to uphold the system. Every kill or capture he'd made since becoming an S/D agent was probably in a way linked to his monster of a father and the gross injustices he had perpetrated. Alpha just didn't like the little guy getting trodden on, he supposed, and the Earth government at Upminster had trodden on more than its fair share. Anyone associated with it, like Dr Francis Persimmion, he deemed tainted as untrustworthy and part of an organisation that had done much to sow division and stigmatise other human beings. He was, he knew, being unfair and bringing his own prejudices to bear. To tar them all with the same brush wasn't a million miles away from what his psychopathic old dad had tried to achieve.

He looked back at Wulf. The big man's company these past few months had definitely softened his antipathy towards norms, made him question his own assumptions. He could never have anticipated how influential their friendship would be, each of them proving a tonic for the other. "Okay, you win," he said finally. "Wait here, I'll go after her."

Johnny jogged out into the corridor, presuming that Fran was going to be on her way back to the shuttle port; she didn't have that much of a head start on him, he was sure he could catch up with her before she left the Doghouse. As it happened, his partner had been right on another count too – he found the woman in conversation with a pair of dubious Stronts, Nerder and Plank, who had a well-deserved reputation amongst their colleagues for bottom-feeding in the pursuit of a cash reward. She couldn't have picked a sleazier duo.

"Doctor Persimmion," Johnny called out as he approached them. They all turned, her eyes registering surprise and relief, the two mutants curling their lips in displeasure.

"Flake off, Alpha," Plank snarled. "We're discussin' business here."

"Doctor," Johnny continued, ignoring the other two, "I've changed my mind. I'd like to make my services available to you, if you're still interested."

"Well, uh..." she answered uncertainly, motioning to the agents at her side.

"Yeah, take a hike," Nerder growled, stepping closer.

Alpha stood his ground, smiling. "You are, of course, at liberty to hire whomever you please, Doctor. But I feel beholden to point out that Plank here is under investigation for an incident on Xantill involving an entire village that disappeared. Got the blast radius wrong on your time bomb, wasn't it?"

"Nothin' was proved, snecker—"

"Until the trial, anyway."

"Y'know, not everyone here thinks you're such a big-shot, Alpha," Nerder spat, poking an excessively long digit in the centre of Johnny's chest. "You wanna be real careful—"

"Oh, I will," Johnny replied, grabbing Nerder's fingers with one hand and twisting them back, forcing the yelping mutant to his knees, while simultaneously sliding his blaster from its holster and pointing it in Plank's flat face. "In fact, I'm taking pre-emptive action – you two, make yourselves scarce. Now."

The pair of Stronts scrambled away, ridiculed by a few other chuckling agents who'd watched the whole scene, and Alpha turned back to a mildly shocked Fran. "Sorry about that. Believe me, it was doing you a favour." He slid the Westinghouse home. "You need a Dog you can trust."

She nodded, visibly grateful. Concern was still etched on her features.

He beckoned her back to the suite. "So let's talk."

Chapter Three

JOHNNY HAD PASSED through collapsing solar systems with more ease than getting out of Hegley customs. His and Wulf's shuttle had been tracked and escorted the moment it entered the moon's airspace, and they'd been put in a holding pattern for a good hour before they were given permission to land. Upon disembarking, they were met by the unsmiling faces of several local cops, who promptly marched them off to an immigration tank, clearly earmarked for undesirables, and had their weapons confiscated and luggage diligently searched. It came as zero surprise to Alpha when the two S/D agents were repeatedly informed that their presence was unwelcome, and a mutant even more so. He encountered this kind of reaction with such regularity that he became more suspicious when he was greeted with open arms; but the antagonistic language was usually silenced with a flash of his GCC warrant card. Police forces were charged under galactic law to accept that Strontium Dogs were licensed to operate on their territory. As Johnny had predicted, however, with no bounty in place on the head of a wanted criminal, they had a legal status little better than tourists; he'd tried to argue the case that they were sanctioned observers, employed in a private capacity, but that didn't cut much ice with those that evidently took great pleasure in telling a Stront where to go.

They were stonewalled for half a day, their requests to leave the spaceport flat-out refused – ostensibly because they were told that their IDs were being double-checked and their records investigated, but Johnny figured they were simply trying to discourage the agents from pursuing the case, wearing them down in the hope they'd hop straight back on their shuttle and return to the Doghouse. He'd experienced so many of these tinpot colonies with their small-town mentalities that he'd become conversant with their predictable and unsubtle methods, and bore them with gritted teeth, aware that mutie-haters only needed the slightest provocation – a raised voice, a threatening word – to unleash a world of hurt. Better to take the path of least resistance, to avoid confrontation when it was unnecessary, if they didn't want their stay on Hegley to be challenged every step of the way. However, while Alpha may have grown used to it, Wulf was almost permanently on a hair-trigger: not yet adept at dealing with the petty bureaucratic machinations of planetoids like this, he looked close to wading in with his fists on more than one occasion. Johnny had allowed himself a small smile when he'd seen the terrified expression cross the officers' faces as an angry Viking took a step towards them. A quiet word from Alpha and he backed off, growling, tipping his partner a surreptitious wink to acknowledge he was fully in tune with the game being played.

Eventually, they were seen by Everson, Hegley's chief of police. A portly, bilious man, he managed to somehow simultaneously exude self-importance and a crushing awareness of his own ineptitude. He was out of his depth, and obviously tried to stave it off by reasserting his authority at every opportunity. He sneered and strutted, luxuriating in the situation. A pair of cops hovered at his shoulder, nervously fingering the tasers in their belts.

"You say you've been hired by Persimmion's wife," he muttered, flapping several sheets of paper before him, running an eye over them theatrically. The documents presumably showed Johnny and Wulf's statements, which they'd given what felt like a century ago, and really didn't need further corroboration. "She not with you?"

"No," Alpha replied patiently. "It was considered she'd be safer if she stayed back on Earth." This was true: despite Fran's protestations that she wanted to join them after Iris's funeral, the

S/D agents had been unequivocal on that point. Hegley was too dangerous right now, and they would work more efficiently if they didn't have her to worry about.

"How much is she paying you?"

"That's none of your business."

Everson chuckled sourly. "At the moment, you *are* my business, mutant, so I suggest you answer my questions if you don't want to see the inside of a cell."

Johnny sighed. "A thousand a day."

"Each?"

"Between us."

The police chief whistled, scanning the sheets again, pursing his lips. After a brief pause, he said: "Like leeching off the desperate, do you, Alpha?"

"I don't follow," he answered, knowing all too well where this line of questioning was going.

"You Strontium Dogs, chasing your blood money. Once you get it in your nostrils, there's no stopping you, is there? Hundreds of you freaks scattered across the galaxy, all trying to collect your bounties, hunting men down like animals. Nothing you won't do for the right fee, is there?"

"We're freelance operatives, if that's what you mean."

"Shameful, shameful," he muttered, shaking his head, "the way your kind exploit tragedies like this. A woman loses her daughter, her husband is unaccounted for, and here you come sniffing around, seeing what creds you can wring from her grief-stricken state."

"Der doctor approached *us*," Wulf growled. "She hired us to find him. Ve're taking advantage of no one."

"Except that at the moment Xander Persimmion is being treated as a fugitive, and is wanted for questioning." Everson had to look up to meet Wulf's eye. "His wife should never have got mercenaries like you involved, and you should've realised that this is a case best left for the authorities instead of chasing a payday."

"Maybe she didn't have much faith in der authorities, und who can blame her—"

"Listen, Sven," the police chief rapped the rolled-up papers against Wulf's chest, who looked down at them with a thunderous expression, "I dunno what ice-floe you've just stepped off, but you want to watch that mouth of yours, understand? Keep a sock in it, 'less you're looking for trouble." Everson turned to Alpha, jerking his head at the Viking. "Where'd you find the Beast of the Fjords, anyway? Only norm I've ever seen working as a Stront." He spat the last word as if it left a bad taste in his mouth.

"Wulf's my partner," Johnny replied testily, "and since neither of us are criminals and our credentials obviously check out, I would appreciate it if you treated us with a little respect and sent us on our way."

"I've got every right, Alpha, to boot you boys back to that flying freakshow you muties call home."

"Except, if you did so, you know that we'd simply sub-contract the job – split the reward with some of our colleagues from that flying freakshow and bring them back here. Maybe a couple of shuttles' worth, at least. Far easier, I would've thought, to keep tabs on just a pair of agents than a whole busload of mutants out for bother."

Everson exhaled angrily, staring at Johnny for long moments. "They clean?" he barked over his shoulder at one of his subordinates.

"All the paperwork's up to date. Nothing more to hold them with."

"Fine. Okay, Alpha, you and the grizzly can go. But we'll be monitoring your movements, believe me."

"Our weapons?"

"You have a right to bear arms on Hegley. You'll get your hardware back." He glanced at the flunkey again. "Neumann, take them through." Then, as the bounty hunters filed out, he called: "Watch your step, mutie. Plenty looking for a fight. Whole town is wired right now. First sign of aggro and you'll be behind bars."

"Not a good start, huh, Johnny?" Wulf whispered, snatching his Happy Stick back from a cop struggling to lift it.

Alpha didn't answer, checking his blaster was fully charged before holstering it.

ON AT LEAST one point Everson had been right: the place was buzzing. The colony – also called Hegley, there being no differentiation in the eyes of the humans between the moon and the cluster of domed buildings that was the Terran occupation; naturally, the native Banabloos had a whole host of names for their home and the five other satellites circling the dead world of Bannas – was cramped and overcrowded. The narrow thoroughfares weren't built for the number of people packing them, and the buildings were cheaply constructed, thrown together in a rush. It certainly wasn't for the scenery that they were coming here – Hegley was for the most part an ugly, dusty hole; quite why the med-council summit had chosen it was a mystery – but it was rich in valuable ores and metals, and that made it an attractive strip n' dip destination for every two-bit mining outfit that could brave the sulphurous stink and howling winds of the plains beyond the city. As Johnny and Wulf edged their way through the throng, they saw the rock-jockeys everywhere filling the bars, in heated conversations with company suits, and staggering out of fast-food outlets – they were identifiable by the grey coating that clung to their skin, some tainted a light blue, a peculiarity of being exposed to the moon's gases in certain areas.

If Hegley's miner districts were always jumping, then post-shuttle crash there was a whole other atmosphere. Still they drank and caroused, but now it had a taint of violence, a shortness of temper. It seemed like all of them had lost someone they knew when the ship exploded, and they were hungry for a villain, a hate figure, to direct their ire at. Xander Persimmion was the current favourite, and even though no one had yet uncovered any evidence that pointed the finger at him – much less his motivation – his face was an almost permanent fixture on the flatscreens behind every bar or mounted amongst the billboards. Drunkenly posited accusations filled the air, most of them insisting Persimmion was in league with the aliens. The populace was bitter and surly, and inevitably strangers were viewed highly suspiciously and were a target for intoxicated intimidation.

Johnny had been down this road plenty of times and brushed off the random insults in the manner of a seasoned professional, having neither the time nor the inclination to square off against half the colony. Wulf, on the other hand, had yet to become fully accustomed to the outright hostility the norms displayed towards mutants, and looked at Alpha questioningly as the agents circumvented another potential confrontation.

"Vot is their problem?" he asked.

"Old habits, I guess. You can get as far as you like from Earth, but the attitudes don't change."

"But doesn't it make you angry? How can you not vant to smash some faces?"

"Sure. When I was younger, maybe I would've took them all on, made them pay for every jibe. That approach only gets you so far, and you don't win any new converts, just more enemies. These days I pick my battles."

"*Pah!* All I see are voorms that could do with a taste of der Happy Stick."

"That's as maybe, big fella," Alpha said, putting a hand on Wulf's shoulder, "but remember why we're here – we don't want to start undue trouble if we can help it, not with Everson breathing down our necks."

"So ve just ignore them, allow them to say vot they vant? Back home, I vould be vearing their gizzards by now."

"It's just fear; that's what at the heart of it. They're scared of what's different, and fear turns into anger and distrust. You Vikings weren't that dissimilar, I seem to recall."

"But if a man proved himself in combat, then he could vin respect, vherever he came from. You did so yourself, Johnny. You showed me you vere a noble, strong fighter by dint of your actions, not vot you looked like."

"Yeah, well, looks like everyone here's taking it all at face value. Presuming he's still alive, Persimmion's guilt is a foregone conclusion. The whole moon's turned into a lynch mob."

"Dey are saying that der natives are involved, these..." Wulf searched for the word.

"Banabloos, yeah. That's got me thinking – what if he *did* have some connection to them? They'd be the ideal friends to hide you, if you needed them to."

"But der police, they have already searched der alien townships..."

"I'm not filled with confidence regarding Hegley police's abilities. It wouldn't be difficult to keep something from them, should the 'bloos be so inclined."

"You think he *is* guilty, then?"

"My instinct says no. But if he survived the explosion, it could be that the Banabloos took him in, kept him out of sight. It wouldn't be easy for a lone fugitive to escape the attention of a whole colony without help."

"So... vot? Ve talk to der aliens?"

Alpha nodded. "I figure they're going to be more receptive than the norms, certainly. We'll check in to a motel, then head on out." He skirted around another expletive-bellowing drunk that had made a beeline for the pair and swayed unsteadily before them, eyes unfocused. Wulf couldn't resist prodding him in chest with his warhammer as he went by and watching with some satisfaction as the man tumbled arse-backwards onto the street, incomprehension painted on his slack features.

THE BANABLOO TOWNSHIPS were an addendum to the colony itself, a ramshackle collection of dwellings shored up against the human walls like they were trying to huddle closer for warmth. Once you got past these rudimentary buildings you were out into the Hegley wastes proper. Though there were plenty of the indigenous population still living off the land as their ancestors had done for millennia, here the 'bloos had to a degree turned their backs on their past and sought to ingratiate themselves with the colonists. It was a sad state of affairs when a good proportion of the natives, whose race had effectively been turfed off their own territory, were desperate to curry favour with their usurpers as they looked for work, or simply sought equal standing socially. They were an intelligent species, if easily impressed, but too many of them seemed to embrace victimhood, or were willing to kowtow to the bipeds from Earth. The aliens weren't barred from entering the human enclave – a small percentage found employment amongst the colonists, their strength and servile nature proving useful – but they weren't actively encouraged either. Hegley wasn't big on integration; maybe having the 'bloos under their noses made the Earthers feel guilty, or perhaps they were simply too ugly for their delicate sensibilities to stomach. Whichever, the natives clearly inspired much the same feelings that muties did in norms: happy for them to do their dirty work, but didn't want them living in close proximity. Naturally, humans rarely, if ever, went into the townships.

Given that it was an area generally avoided by everyone, it was testament to how high feelings were currently riding that a small group of inebriated miners were hanging round the entrance to the Banabloo reservation, bottle in one hand, blaster in the other. They were demanding that the 'bloos give Persimmion up, as well as any of the aliens he was in league with, before they stormed in and dragged him out themselves. A representative of the native people was standing at the threshold, calmly preventing their entry, shaking its head and repeating that the wanted man was not here. A bottle was thrown, and the 'bloo had to swiftly duck. Alpha had seen enough.

"On your way," he snarled, "before you idiots kill somebody."

"Get lost, freak," one of them retorted. "Ain't none of your business."

"Our business now," Wulf said, grabbing the colonist by the back of his collar and lifting him off his feet. "You vant to make more of it?"

"Drop him," came a yell, and guns were being raised. Before Johnny even had a chance to issue a warning, the Viking's warhammer had left his outstretched hand and flown into the nearest figure's chest, driving him onto his back. The mutant flicked on his electronux and waded into the fray, laying out the remainder while they were still drunkenly trying to aim; they went down hard and didn't stir. To be on the safe side, the agents collected up the miners' weapons and dismantled them, throwing the firing mechanisms into the undergrowth.

"Thank you," the 'bloo said.

Alpha nodded in acknowledgement, aware of how little time they had – if they didn't find Persimmion quickly, the townships could end up torched. The pair drew more than a few stares as they strode into the alien sector. Banabloos weren't, admittedly, the most attractive of species – dung-brown running to black, multi-limbed, and insectoid, they resembled two-metre tall centipedes with disarmingly benign faces, their dark, button-like eyes exuding empathy and understanding. Alpha had seen enough of the galaxy to be inured to its oddities, but he could feel Wulf bristling next to him, uncomfortable under their gaze and struggling not to make his revulsion plain. The buildings were constructed from mud and vegetation, a cross between huts and giant anthills, and the curious aliens scuttled between them, pouring in and out of the huts' apertures as they kept pace with the newcomers. Eventually, one of them reared up in front of the agents, impenetrable ebony orbs regarding them unblinking.

"You are bounty hunters," it said, its voice a clicking whisper, mandibles weirdly as expressive as lips.

"That's right," Johnny answered, noticing from the corner of his eye his partner's hand resting on the butt of his holstered Webley. "We're—"

"You are here for the missing dead man," it interjected. "From the night it rained fire."

"We've been hired by his wife, yes, who believes him to still be alive."

"Police have already been here, looking for him. We told them we do not know where he is."

"I'm aware of that. But we're not from the colony, we don't represent Hegley. We're trying to find Xander Persimmion as much to save him from execution at the hands of the authorities as to reunite him with his spouse. As long as the police are looking for him, his life is in danger."

"Our thoughts are with all those that lost lives," it said, bowing its head and putting several feet together as if it was offering up a brief prayer. "We saw wreckage fall from here, heard screams, wail of sirens. It was darkest time we've ever known on Bantarr, since humans arrived. We offered to help but they sealed off area – they say we were not to interfere." It paused, gazing beyond the two men for a moment, sadness casting a shadow over its features. "We hope doctor is safe, but many souls – including his child's – rest in balance until he found: they cannot be released until the circle is closed. For that, the humans must act as they see fit." It sounded like a rehearsed mantra that it used to convince itself, a delusional insistence that they should trust the Earthers to do the right thing.

"Did you hear what those cretins at the gates were threatening to do? The colonists are blaming Banabloo factions; you do realise that, don't you?" Alpha said. Its oily voice had set him on edge.

"They won't hesitate to pin this on your people and use it as a wedge to drive you further off your land."

"They have given assurances—"

"Their word means nothing if they feel they're under attack. They'll stamp down on you, and stamp hard. If you know something about Persimmion's whereabouts, then you're not helping yourselves by protecting him."

"We do not know where he is," it repeated uncertainly.

Alpha wasn't slow to pick it up. "Wait, you know he had a daughter. You've *met* him, at least, haven't you? Did he come here, on a prior visit?"

It thought for a second then nodded reluctantly. "A rotation ago, he meet us. Said he wanted to see where we lived."

"In the township?"

"Across Bantarr. We show him our map."

Johnny and Wulf glanced at each other. "Can we see it?" the mutant asked.

It dipped its head. "I can trust you?"

"You going to have to if you want your people to survive this."

It considered this, looking to its fellows as if silently conversing with them. Alpha could glean nothing from its head. "Come," it said. It turned and slithered quickly away, the agents having to jog to catch up with it as it scuttled into a particularly tall structure in the centre of the community, blazing torches affixed to its walls. Naturally, the rest of the 'bloos followed, crowding outside. Within, the orange, flicking light illuminated a vast painting decorating one side – it was a crude but detailed depiction of the entire Hegley wastelands, crosses and markings and notes intricately included amongst the mountain ranges and desert fields. "Here we track our kin, those that choose not to live with the humans," the alien murmured. Clearly this was a place of great importance, where voices were suitably lowered. "We chart where each clan makes its home, the better to bind us together."

"And Persimmion was interested in this?" Johnny said.

"He looked at it for long time."

Wulf leaned in to Alpha's ear. "Vot you thinking?" he whispered. "He was trying to find somewhere to hide?"

"Maybe. If so, he was planning this a *year* before the explosion."

It was late by the time the two of them were making the way back into Hegley and towards their motel.

"Der creatures are a funny bunch," Wulf commented.

"Yeah, almost like they've been bullied into accepting humans as their masters, who do no wrong. Plenty of the 'bloos living out in the wastes feel differently, though."

"They are der activists?"

"And it could be that that's who Persimmion is in league with. Looking like he might've been responsible for the explosion, after all."

"But his child—"

"A mistake, perhaps. She could've meant to have survived it too, but something went wrong."

The Viking shook his head. "Ach, this is not right. No father could—"

The shot rang out, sharp and sudden, cutting him short. Wulf grunted, stumbled, then dropped to his knees, blood pooling in the dust beneath him.

Chapter Four

Johnny crouched next to his friend, who had one hand planted on the ground to stop him collapsing face-first; his other was held tightly to his chest in a bid to stem the flow of blood. He breathed through gritted teeth, his eyes squeezed shut as if concentrating on managing the burning sensation tearing across his nerve-endings, but Alpha could see him weakening, and moments later his supporting arm wobbled and gave out, dropping him with a hiss of pain. The mutant turned his partner onto his back and planted both of his hands on the entry wound, just to the right of his sternum, and told him to keep them there. A crimson puddle was forming beneath him; clearly, the slug had passed all the way through, punching out somewhere near his kidneys. Even if he'd got lucky and avoided any organ damage, he was going to bleed out unless he received medical attention.

"Okay, big guy, keep the pressure on that wound," Alpha said. Wulf's face was sheened with sweat, and his chest was rising and falling rapidly. Johnny looked around, hoping to catch a glimpse of anyone that could raise the alarm, but the area was deserted; it was an industrial wasteground somewhere between the Banabloo reservation and the populated lower district, and sparsely lit – a perfect spot for a hit, and he admonished himself for not being more on his guard. Their enemies, it seemed, were tripling by the hour, and they should've anticipated trouble.

Just as he ducked forward to check the Viking's pulse, the second shot chipped Alpha's helmet and buried itself into a nearby squat wall, part of a half-demolished building. He drew his blaster and flattened himself on the earth, parallel to Wulf, who moved his head slightly to look his partner in the eye.

"Who are dey?" he gasped, every word sounding as if it was sandpapering his lungs.

"Don't know yet," Johnny whispered, scanning the darkness, alpha-ray enhanced vision penetrating the gloom to reveal the possible silhouettes of three figures ahead. "Wait… Think I can see 'em, positioned in the scrub. They knew we were coming back this way, were lying in wait. Professionals, too, judging by the accuracy of the shots."

"Not a… random attack, then?"

"No, this was meant for us. Somebody's targeted us for assassination."

"Vot's" – he grimaced – "the plan?"

"Gotta end this quick and get you to a hospital. Maybe I could flank them…"

"No damn hospital. I don't trust them."

"We haven't got a choice, pal. We don't get you to a doc, you're heading for Valhalla."

"Vulf has had vurse," he started, trying to pull himself up, but Johnny gently pushed him back down. Another shot hit the ground raising a plume of dirt inches from his head.

"I doubt it; that's no scrape from a battleaxe. C'mon, let's find you cover." He dragged a cursing Wulf a few feet until he was mostly shielded by the wall. "Listen: I'm gonna draw their fire. You stay put, Okay? Don't ease up on the pressure or you'll start to lose consciousness."

His partner snorted in response, but Alpha didn't stay any longer to argue. Keeping low against the ground and using elbows and knees to propel himself, he snaked his way off to the right, keeping an eye on the figures to see if they were tracking him; it was more than likely that they were using scoped weapons, possibly infra-red. A rake of gunfire following in his wake confirmed it. The upper hand was theirs, he knew, and they were going to pick the both of them off before too long unless he evened the playing field a touch. He paused, sighted the Westinghouse above the area their attackers were centred and fired off a flare round – the ball of iridescence bloomed wide and white in the starless sky, the sudden stark light flattening the shadows and dispelling the night. It revealed the gunmen like a beacon, arms thrown over eyes and tearing off IR goggles with barks of distress.

They were crudely masked – scarves wrapped around their lower faces, caps pulled tightly down on their heads – and they were dressed in featureless dark camo gear; Alpha could tell nothing from their appearance as to who they were or who they were affiliated with. But he'd been right: they had the air of professionals, and judging by the nondescript combat clothes and the way they held themselves and their weaponry – Gunterlich automatic rifles, he guessed, which weren't exactly standard issue out here in the boondocks, plus each of them had a holstered sidearm – it was clear that these weren't drunk colonists out to bag a mutie or local far-right militia, but seasoned triggermen, hired by persons unknown to wipe the S/D agents out. It made things easier for him, at least; an idiot shooting randomly into the night he might hold back on, and aim to disable or disarm. No such reticence when the opponent was a contract killer.

Alpha stood and pressed home the advantage while the hitmen were still disorientated in the diminishing glow of the dying flare: he snapped off two shots and caught the nearest figure in the shoulder and neck, blowing away a good proportion of his throat. The other two panicked when their comrade's blood sprayed across them and swung their rifles to bear and let loose, pumping recoilless rounds in Johnny's direction, but the Stront was already moving, heading for cover in another of the abandoned buildings. A bulletstorm smashed into the nearside wall just as he dived behind it. The sheer intensity of the onslaught made him catch his breath for a second and wonder briefly what exactly he and Wulf had done to warrant such relentless determination. Was the assassins' intention to bring their investigations into Persimmion's whereabouts to a quiet halt? If so, they were giving up the clandestine approach and going for all-out assault. It would hopefully bring down the Hegley police – even they couldn't turn a deaf ear to an exchange of automatic gunfire – and increase Wulf's chances of making it to a med-centre in time, but until they arrived his own chances of survival were fading by the second. They were piling it on and no doubt advancing on his position; he could hear them conferring between bursts, and he caught enough to establish that they were from Earth and that they knew who he was. He wasn't just a target, a name on a hitlist – the way they talked about him it sounded as if they knew him personally. His curiosity piqued, he suddenly had an urge to take one of them alive, and find out just who the hell they were.

Right now, that seemed a luxury he couldn't afford. The retort of their fire suggested that they were approaching from two different sides, narrowing his angle of escape. Time was running out. He cocked his head to one side when he realised there was a pause in the barrage coming from his right; the guy was reloading. He took the chance and clambered to his feet, dashing further into the building. The gunman looked up from clicking home a fresh magazine and shouted to his compatriot, who swung his rifle in Johnny's direction and unleashed a burst after him. Alpha slalomed into an adjoining room, ricochets pinging off the brickwork behind him, and spun around when he discovered there was nowhere further to go; it had evidently been a storage shed of some description, and wasn't especially large. He backed against the far wall, watching the shadows of the two figures dance across the stone floor as they passed over the threshold. Any... minute... now.

The dull *whump* sounded like a grenade going off underground: a contained, bass-heavy discharge that nevertheless barely shook the dust motes drifting in the air. There'd been a brief scream, which was unusual – normally, time bombs detonated so instantaneously there was no reaction at all from those trapped within its field. He edged towards the front of the building, casting a cursory eye over the shallow crater left by the weapon's explosion; he'd left it on short timer, allowing just long enough for his assailants to pass into its vicinity. Trapped within its blast radius, victims of time bombs were frozen in a moment of time and left to perish in the void of space as the bubble remained stationary and the planet moved on.

So much for learning more about who they were, he thought, but he had to admit it had been the quickest solution to his situation.

Johnny was aware of red and blue lights flashing and the distant sound of sirens as he headed over to the body of the third hitman and yanked away his scarf and cap – he was human, unremarkable and unrecognisable. Alpha swiftly patted him down, conscious that the cops would be at the scene imminently, but his pockets were empty; no ID whatsoever. Another sign of a professional soldier.

"Stand down! I repeat: stand down!" The megaphone-enhanced voice rose above the clamour of the sirens.

He backed away quickly as the first of the police vehicles nosed its way onto the wasteground and was in the process of jogging his way back to where he'd left Wulf when he felt something tighten around his ankle and tug violently on his leg, tripping him up; he crashed to the dusty ground, wondering if in the darkness his foot had got caught in a pothole. He twisted round, setting his electronux to glow so he could see better, and realised that someone was crawling up him, hands grasping his thighs. It was one of the gunmen; or rather, it was *half* of one of the gunmen, as his body ended at his waist. There was no blood, no smear of viscera, just an absence below the torso as if his legs had been erased. Johnny knew instantly what had happened – the hitman must've been on the edge of the time bomb's field and only his lower body had been vaporised. He'd been the source of the scream. The scarf was still wrapped around his lower face, but he'd lost his cap and Alpha could see enough of his glazed eyes, lit green from the electronux, to judge that his sanity had gone somewhere south too. The mutant tried to push him away, and when he found his assailant's grip was unbreakable he pounded on the side of the man's head in a bid to dislodge him, but to no avail. The hitman knocked Johnny's hand to one side and managed to get his fingers to his throat, pressing deep into his larynx; Alpha attempted to free his Westinghouse from its holster, but it was trapped beneath him.

Stars danced before his eyes as he struggled to breathe. The man seemed to have supernatural strength, as if the shock of his injury had lent him a machine-like remorselessness, his blank face betraying no emotion. Nothing Alpha did could shake him off, nor could he tear his hands from his neck. It occurred to him that the police weren't that far away, and if he could only muster enough air to shout out to them, they could come to his assistance – but his choked cries barely escaped his lips. The pressure on his throat deepened, his head overloading with pain and panic.

Johnny felt the cool swirl of a breeze above his face momentarily before the weight on his chest suddenly eased and his constricted throat was loosened. He gasped instinctively, drawing in deep lungfuls, and his darkening eyes focused: standing beside him was a huge bearded man, swaying slightly with one arm wrapped across his chest, and using the warhammer clutched in the other for support.

"Johnny? You are okay?" he rumbled.

"Wulf?" Alpha croaked. He gently rubbed his sore neck, swallowed several times. "How... how the hell are you still standing?"

The Viking shrugged. "Told you I'd had vurse." He reached down and offered a hand, though he was decidedly shaky pulling the mutant to his feet. Between the two of them they managed to stand. Alpha looked down and saw the remains of the gunman lying on his side, his skull caved in behind the ear.

"Ach, vot a mess," Wulf muttered. "Der Happy Stick had to intervene again."

"Thanks, big fella. That's one I owe you."

"Is nothing." He nodded to the corpse. "You recognise them?"

"No, never seen them before."

"Somebody hired dem, that's for sure."

"Offworld contract killers, I'm certain of it. If someone wants us dead this badly, and is getting outside help to do it, I reckon we need to find them before they try again." He studied Wulf's bloodied jerkin and pale complexion; even his obstinate bravado couldn't mask how urgently he needed medical treatment. "But right now we've got to get you sorted out."

"I think dey might vant a vord first," his partner replied, motioning to the squad of armed cops bearing down on them, torches playing across the scene.

"Ah. Yeah, this could take some explaining."

*　　*　　*

CHIEF EVERSON WAS, not unpredictably, less than happy to see them again so soon. "I figured you two for trouble-magnets. I'll admit I didn't expect the body count to start on the first night."

"Hardly our fault if we're made a target."

The policeman grunted, clearly unconvinced. He and Alpha were standing in a waiting room in a med-facility in the upper districts, Everson wisely deciding that it was more likely that they would receive treatment uninterrupted further they were from the rock-jockeys. Johnny had been checked over for the bruising around his neck, and once it had been established that he'd escaped any serious damage to his windpipe he was discharged; Wulf, on the other hand, was being kept overnight to recuperate after emergency surgery. Fortunately, the bullet had passed through him reasonably cleanly, and it was mainly blood loss and wound sterilisation that the doctors were concerned about. They told him his body needed time to heal itself, for which rest was required, but the Viking, true to his nature, grumbled about even this. Even though he doubted his partner would admit it, Alpha detected an appreciation on Wulf's part for the speed of 23rd-century medicine: the organ scans, booster shots and auto-stitching meant he felt better a hell of a lot quicker than the long periods of recovery he would've had to endure – where risk of infection and death were ever-present – back in his own time. He was a great bear of a man who projected an innate sense that nothing could kill him – perhaps ingrained since childhood, since all warriors had to believe that was so – but surely even he had to be aware occasionally of his own mortality. The two had known each other now for several months, but Johnny still underestimated Wulf's tenacity, bravery and stoic resolve. It had staggered him that the Viking had managed to find the strength to come to his aid; he simply didn't know how he'd got to his feet, what resources he'd drawn on. The two had pulled each other's fat out of the fire plenty of times since they'd become partners, and Alpha had always been comfortable relying on him to have his back, but this was possibly the first time he'd experienced what the Viking was capable of. His bullishness was a wonder to behold when the chips were down.He couldn't bring himself to return to their motel, but preferred to spend what remained of the early hours in the waiting room adjacent to Wulf's private ward. Any concerns he may have had about further attacks were leavened by the presence of a couple of cops on the door, who were preventing anyone but nursing staff from entering, but it also meant he had to suffer the company of Everson, who'd been interrogating him solidly about the night's events. Alpha could tell that the police chief had long concluded that this wasn't a firefight that the Search/Destroy agents had instigated, and that there was nothing to charge them or deport them with, but nevertheless he disliked bounty hunters in his town enough to give the mutant a grilling anyway.

"You got an ID on the attackers yet?" Johnny asked.

Everson shook his head. "The one still pretty much in one piece is with the coroner now, but we haven't had the report back. We'll be lucky to get much off the torso Sven caved in the skull of – fingerprints, maybe." He smiled unpleasantly. "Budget won't extend to a deep-space retrieval mission for the third, I'm afraid."

The mutant ignored the comment. "They were hired professionals, lying in wait for us. Almost certainly offworld contractors paid to take us out – which suggests that there are parties on Hegley who are aware we're here and are seeking to stop our investigation."

"Alpha, *I'm* not happy you're here – and you're not legally entitled to conduct any investigation, as you've been told before. The search for Persimmion remains under the remit of the colony police."

"Since we've been targeted for murder, I'd say it just became a criminal matter, which an S/D agent has the right to pursue if he feels his life is in danger."

Everson sighed. "You're a real ballache, you know that, don't you, Stront? Listen to me: stay out of our way. We'll follow up any leads on the hit-team, understand? I hear about you two going all guns blazing into another shootout, and I'll have you locked up in max-sec until the Persimmion case is over. I won't have you snecking mutie cowboys running rampant on Hegley."

"If the trouble comes looking for us, Everson, we don't have much choice."

"I'm giving you your choices, boy," the police chief replied, fixing Johnny with a glare before stalking out of the room. "Just so there's no ambiguity. You're not welcome here," he called out as he disappeared down the corridor, "and if you do stay I better not hear a peep from you."

Alpha slumped down into a chair and removed his helmet, studying the nick on it that the bullet had grazed before tossing it onto a nearby seat. He closed his eyes, fatigue gnawing at his bones.

Wulf responded well to the rapid-heal treatment and was released by noon the following day. The docs had done a decent job patching him up but he was still sore, and, Johnny thought as they walked back to their digs, unusually quiet. He winced every now and then, his hand automatically going to his wound.

"You okay?" Johnny asked.

"Ja, ja. So vot now?"

"I need to track who was behind those gunmen. Screw Everson – we can't wait for them to take another shot at us." They entered the motel lobby and headed for the elevators. "You might want to sit this one out, pal – wait until you've fully recovered."

"Ach, I'm fine, I—"

"Mr Alpha." The soft female voice came from behind them, and they both turned, momentarily silenced. Dr Frances Persimmion was hesitantly approaching them, having risen from one of the sofas placed near the building's reception area.

"I've been waiting for you," she said.

Chapter Five

THEY HELD OFF on the inevitable barrage of questions until they had shepherded Fran into an elevator and up to Alpha's room. Once the door was shut, he rounded on her, his face dark.

"What the hell are you doing here?"

She looked taken aback, a little fearful. "I... I couldn't stop thinking about what was happening here, about where Xander was. With the funeral over, I had nothing to do but dwell on the shuttle crash, speculate on what they'd do to my husband if he was still alive. I couldn't eat, couldn't sleep... I felt I needed to be doing something or I would start losing my grip entirely..."

"You realise how dangerous Hegley is right now? That is why you hired us – to search for Xander on your behalf so you wouldn't have to enter this warzone."

"I know... I suppose I just couldn't wait."

"We *settled* this," Johnny exclaimed angrily. "We agreed that you would stay on Earth, that the colony wasn't safe for a civilian. Having you here compromises our position, means we have *you* to protect as well as ourselves."

"I'm sorry, I thought I could help."

"The best way you could've helped was to stay at home and wait for us to call."

"Do you know what that's *like*?" Fran snapped, taking a step closer to Johnny, unflinching in her glare. "To spend every waking moment waiting for news, sitting there, staring at the com, willing it to put you out of your misery? Feeling trapped, paralysed, unable to concentrate on anything because a part of your mind is constantly churning through possibilities?" Her eyes dropped to the floor, her voice lowered. "I've lost my daughter, and I may well have lost my husband too – but until I know for sure, I can't ever settle. If he's dead and his body needs bringing home, or he's alive and he needs protection, I should be here for him. Better here than chained to the com, every minute crawling by..."

There was a pause. "How did you get through security?" Alpha asked. "Once they saw your surname, I'm surprised they didn't hold you for questioning – or use you to try to bring your husband in."

"I flew in under my maiden name – I'm not stupid. No one here but you two knows who I am."

Johnny sighed. "You better hope it stays that way. Anyone finds out who you are, it's going to pour yet more fuel on the fire. They'll think you're in league with Xander, that you know where he is and you've come to get him off-world. The way feelings are running right now, the moment your identity becomes known you'll become a target."

"It sounds as if you're convinced he's still alive," Fran said, brow furrowed.

"The evidence is pointing that way, let's put it like that. It's been complicated by—"

"Johnny," Wulf interjected with a shake of the head and a stern expression. "Not now."

The doctor looked between the two men. "Is there something I should know? Because let me remind you that I'm the one paying your wages, and if you have information then I suggest you tell me right now."

"Just needs further investigation, is all," Wulf replied. He winced, put his hand to his abdomen and leant against the wall.

"My God, are you injured?" Fran exclaimed, rushing to the Viking's side as he raised his other hand to wave her away.

"We came up against one of those complications," Alpha answered.

"What happened?"

"Hitmen, lying in wait to take us out. I can only assume that it's connected to your husband's disappearance and someone doesn't want us pursuing that particular line of inquiry."

"Do you know who they were, who'd sent them?"

"No, but we intend to find out. If I could get a mugshot to the Doghouse, they might have a criminal record on at least one of the men. To be honest, doctor, we were lucky to escape the situation in one piece, though I can't say the same for our attackers. I'll admit, this missing persons case has taken on a whole different shade."

"Wait... you don't think Xander could be behind it? That he genuinely doesn't want to be found?"

"We can't afford to dismiss the possibility."

"No... no," Fran murmured, pacing the length of the room. "No, there's no way he could've been involved in the shuttle explosion. Iris meant everything to him... to us." She brushed away fresh tears. "He wouldn't have done that to her, he wouldn't have been capable. He was a *doctor*, for Christ's sake – why on Earth would he bomb a spaceflight? He'd dedicated his career to saving others, he's not a terrorist!"

"I'm sure you felt you knew your husband, Doctor Persimmion," Alpha replied, "and maybe you're right, maybe he is innocent—"

"Of *course* he's innocent," she retorted angrily. "This is insane. I employed you to find Xander because I thought his life was in danger, and here you are joining the lynch mob."

"We're dealing with the hand that we've been dealt," Johnny said calmly. "What's irrefutable is that someone wants us dead, and that changes matters. Right now, who that is is open to question, and anyone could be a suspect. However, if you wish to dispense with our services, Wulf and I can just as easily hop on the next shuttle out of here. We'll reimburse you what you've already paid us."

She shook her head. "No. No, I want you to stay on the ground looking for him. I need you to." Her face softened. "You're keeping an open mind, I can appreciate that – and you're putting your lives on the line." She looked sympathetically at Wulf. "Thank you. For all you're doing."

"Ach, is nothing," the Viking said. "Johnny, I think I vill take forty vinks, get my strength back."

"Sure."

"You want me to check your dressing?" Fran asked. "I've got some painkillers in my bag."

"Ja, that would be gut. See, Johnny?" he said to his partner with a pained smile as he limped out the door, the doctor in tow. "Having a medic on der team has its benefits."

WULF'S ROOM WAS adjacent to Alpha's, and he eased himself onto his bed, loosening his jerkin and unbuckling his gun holster and laying it carefully on a nearby table. Fran sat beside him and inspected the bandages wrapped round his chest and stomach.

"Still tender, huh?" she said.

He nodded. "I think whatever der hospital gave me must be wearing off."

"It'll take a while for your body to repair itself, even a big guy like you. Still, they've strapped you up well. Here" – she fished in her shoulder bag and pulled out a small, bullet-shaped anaesthetic shot, which she thumbed into his bicep – "that'll take the edge off."

"Is gut," Wulf mumbled as the drug took effect.

"I did a spell in a military infirmary during my student days, seen my fair share of gunshot wounds. Guess it must be an occupational hazard for S/D agents."

"Ja, alvays staring down a barrel. A lot of der voorms ve're hunting are big mouths without der courage to pull der trigger, but then you got der psychos, der ones with nothing to lose..." His voice trailed off, lost in introspection for a moment. "But this... this has been der vorst I've received," he said quietly, one hand fidgeting at his dressing. "Either back in Norstad or after, partnered with Johnny; I've had my scrapes but this... vas serious. I thought I could hear der call of my ancestors as I lay there. I properly felt fear."

"You stayed with Mr Alpha rather than return to your people, didn't you? I did some research after our first meeting, read about the time-job he was sent on, where you two met. It was a huge step you took, to become what you are now – were you not scared then?"

"I had made an oath to Johnny; I did not consider der consequences. I couldn't – der debt I owed him vas too great." Wulf flexed his shoulders, kneading the base of his skull with one meaty hand. "I von't lie and say it's been easy – but no varrior vorth his salt chooses der safe path. It is der challenges that forge us, vouldn't you agree, doctor?"

"You could say that." She smiled sadly. "Mr Alpha – he seems very intense. I don't think he cares much for norms like me."

"Don't take it personally. He has seen enough of how mutants are treated since he vas a boy to be vary around people that aren't his kind. He is guarded, ja. He hasn't told me anything about his past, his family, but it doesn't take a vise man to recognise that he lost a lot, that it's made him who he is. He is a good man, honourable, but you don't get to know much about vot's going on in his head; he keeps it all to himself."

"What about you? What did you leave behind when you became an agent?"

"Ach, a busybody mother and not much else; a couple of vomen, a few comrades that I'll see again in der great drinking hall vhen my time is over. I had no vife, no siblings, no children…" Wulf stopped, glancing at her. "I'm sorry. You have suffered der most terrible tragedy. This" – he gingerly patted his bandaged stomach – "this vill heal in time, der scar vill fade eventually, but vot you have had torn from you vill be vith you alvays. It is der vorst vound of all to lose someone close, but a child? That I don't think I could recover from."

Fran laid a hand on his arm, her eyes glittering. "Right now I don't know if I'll ever come to terms with losing Iris. Every moment I think of her, every memory, is a fresh stab to the heart. I just want to curl up into a ball, close my eyes and never wake up."

"Der life you remember, it should be treasured. It vas joyous vhile it lasted."

"I know. I tell myself to try to not think of what could've been, but concentrate on the time we had together, nurture it. But I feel like I need help sharing the pain, the grief – that's why I'm so desperate to find Xander, to give me someone to cling to. I don't think I can handle it on my own." She sniffed, her voice wavering. "It's all I've got right now: to find him. He's out there, he's alive, I know he is, and I need to bring him home safely."

"Ve'll find him," he assured her, squeezing her hand.

"I appreciate your support, Mr Sternhammer." She was silent for a second, then said: "Don't think that I'm not aware that it was you that convinced Mr Alpha to take my case. You can't imagine how grateful I am for that. I was fast running out of options."

Wulf waved away her words. "I saw a bereaved mother who needed help. So did Johnny – I just had to make him look past der norm thing. It is an issue of trust that he vill admit he has a problem with; as I said, votever happened in his past affected him greatly. He vill learn to be less suspicious in time, I'm sure. But he feels for your plight, I know he does – he vill do everything in his power to help you find your husband. I've never known him give up on a job."

"How much have I screwed things up by being here?"

"Ach, Johnny vos venting. Der adrenaline talking. Ve just need you to keep a low profile, stay out of der firing line. No point tracking down Xander if you're not alive to be reunited."

"I feel so useless; I'm not used to being a spare part. Is there anyway I can help, even if I remain in the background?"

"You have any more of der painkilling shots?"

She smiled. "I do, but you're only meant to take one a day. Is there something more practical I can assist with...?" She stopped, a thought evidently having occurred to her. "Wait... Mr Alpha said that you needed to identify the gunmen that came after you. If the police took away the bodies, then they'll be in the city morgue right now, pending the coroner's report."

"Ja. Der police chief, he told Johnny they were trying to put a name to one of der creeps."

"I know the Hegley coroner – he's attended the medical conferences held here in the past. We're friendly enough that I think I could get one of you into the morgue and take a closer look at the corpse."

"But you vould be exposing yourself—"

"Dendry's discreet; I reckon I can rely on him to keep my presence here a secret. And he's an intelligent guy – he's not one of these kneejerk idiots baying for Xander's blood. He'll have no desire to inform the authorities of my whereabouts."

"Then ve should—" Wulf went to stand and immediately regretted it: one leg wobbled and he sat back down on the bed.

"You need to rest up," Fran told him, making for the door. "Stay here, I'll talk to Mr Alpha. He'll be easier to pass off as a colleague, anyway."

The Viking didn't argue and, stretching out, was snoring within minutes.

DESPITE REITERATING THE risk the doctor was taking, Johnny recognised that her plan could offer them a lead. He stripped off his body armour and slipped on a jacket and tie that he always brought with him on trips when he needed to merge anonymously into a crowd, a pair of shades hiding his mutation. The two of them caught a cab over to the morgue, Fran instructing the woman on the front desk that she wanted to see Dr Dendry and leaving only her first name. They were left waiting only a couple of minutes before a tall, thin, wiry whitecoat with frizzy hair and spectacles emerged, did a double-take at Fran, then quickly ushered him into his office as if he wanted them out of sight.

"Fran? Fran Persimmion?" he said once he'd closed the door. He removed his glasses and squinted at her. "It *is* you, isn't it? You look different..."

"New haircut, maybe. It has been a while. It's good to see you, Marcus. This is John, he's a research assistant of mine."

Alpha shook Dendry's hand; the coroner still looked a touch confused. "Forgive the dark glasses. Light sensitive."

"Sure," he replied distractedly, already turning back to Persimmion. "Fran, Jesus, what are you *doing* here? I mean, I'm so sorry about what happened, I offer my sincere condolences for the loss of your daughter, but they're tearing the colony apart looking for Xander. Do the police know you're on-planet?"

"Of course not, and I'd like it to stay that way. Marcus, please, I'm asking you as a friend that we keep this between ourselves. You know what a knife-edge Hegley's on right now; informing the authorities about my presence is only going to make things worse. I *can* trust you, can't I?"

"Christ..." He rubbed his hands over his face. "Yes, yes, I won't say a word. But you're risking a hell of a lot. Do you... do you know where Xander is?"

"No, not at all, and he hasn't contacted me either, before you ask. I'm here trying to find out what's happened to him, same as everyone else. But I need a big favour – we want to take a look at the body the cops brought in last night."

"The gunman? Why?"

"In case I recognise him. If the shooting was related to the shuttle crash, I want to check he's not someone that I've seen before with Xander."

"You think they're connected? Wait, you don't think Xander *did* cause the explosion? Why would he—"

"I don't know what to think anymore, Marcus. But, please – put my mind at rest. It'll take two seconds. I'm just trying to piece things together, make some sense of what's happened."

"So what's his story?" Dendry said, jerking a thumb at Alpha.

"John was working closely alongside Xander too, the past year. I asked him along to see if the face rings any bells."

"I have to say, if you think your husband's been involved in criminal activity, and the dead guy's part of it, then it's a matter for the police. You'll have to tell them your suspicions."

"I will. But I'd rather not have them jumping to conclusions without anything concrete to go on. You've seen what the mood is like out there."

"It *is* getting crazy," the coroner agreed. "The fire certainly doesn't need any more fuel poured on it."

"The cops must have their theories about what the gunmen were doing here," Johnny said.

"That's not something I'm really at liberty to discuss," Dendry said, dismissively. "By all accounts they specifically targeted two Stronty Dogs that have been sticking their noses in, so it's pretty clear someone – presumably the bomber, whoever that turns out to be – doesn't want the investigation pursued." He turned back to Fran. "The chances of that being Xander, though... It just seems incredible that he could possibly ever do something like this, plan a terrorist act of this nature, get into bed with mutants—"

"What?" Alpha interrupted before he could stop himself.

"If the hitmen were in league with Xander, then he's been consorting with mutants. The guy I've got on the slab out there is no norm."

"Can we see?" Fran asked, sharing a momentary glance with Johnny. "Please?"

Dendry nodded reluctantly. "Come through." He led them out of his office, down a short corridor, through a pair of double doors and into the chill bowels of the morgue. Tables lined its expanse, some empty, most with sheeted corpses lying upon them. There were drawers set into the walls for further body storage.

"You would've handled the bodies from the shuttle disaster?" Alpha said.

"Yes, they came through here. Those we could salvage..." He stopped, shot a look at Fran in apology, and didn't elaborate further. He went up to one of the nearest slabs and without hesitation threw back the sheet covering the body.

The dead man's skin was a waxy yellow, and much work had evidently been done to clean up the neck wound where Johnny's blast had caught him: suture scars criss-crossed his jawline, the back of his skull and his throat. His violent death had been tidied and made presentable; he appeared at peace. However, from first glance – much as Alpha had thought when he pulled the third gunman's scarf away last night – the guy looked normal.

"Do the police know he's a mutant?" Alpha enquired.

"Not yet. I didn't find out myself until just now, and was going to add it into my report. As you can see, he's not obviously mutated." Dendry moved behind the corpse's head and pushed its thick dark hair to one side. "It was in the process of completing the post-mortem that I discovered this."

Fran and Johnny peered closer at the stiff's scalp and saw a pair of small horns, below which was a set of eyes and a mouth, closed in the same serene repose. Surreptitiously, the S/D agent reached into his pocket and retrieved the recording device he'd taken from his helmet back at the motel.

"My God," Fran whispered.

"Yeah, it came as surprise to me too," Dendry murmured. "No ID on him as yet. Have you seen him before?"

"No, never," she replied firmly. "Have you, John?"

"Nope."

The coroner shrugged and pulled the sheet back. "I'm sorry, Fran, I don't know how else I can help you."

"You've done plenty, thanks, Marcus," she said. "I think I was letting my imagination run away with me. We'll get out of your way now."

"DID YOU MANAGE to get a good shot of him?" she asked Johnny when they were standing back out on the street.

"Yeah, it should be enough to go on. I'll upload it to the Doghouse straight away. They might be able to put a name to him."

"You think he'll have an outstanding warrant on him?"

"A warrant? No, the dead guy in there didn't walk out the Milton Keynes ghetto yesterday. The level of weaponry, their accuracy, professionalism..." Alpha paused. "I'm thinking our attackers were Stronts."

Chapter Six

THE BUILDING WAS, in accordance with the aliens' standing with the humans, tiny; a ramshackle, under-maintained structure squeezed on the end of a derelict row in what was laughably supposed to be the cultural centre. It was said that the wealth of towns back on Earth could be judged by the size of their burger franchises; that said, the importance the Hegley colonists placed on the moon's heritage was visible in the state of the Banabloo museum. It was desultory to the point of offensive, a testament to how little the Earthers cared about the species whose world they'd occupied. Johnny imagined they'd only got this because galactic monitoring authorities were supposed to be keeping an eye upon the treatment and representation of all sentient life forms, but clearly the barest level of effort had been expended. That didn't surprise him in the least. What still mystified him was the passive way in which the Banabloos accepted their environment's exploitation, and even seemed weirdly grateful for it, as if they'd been waiting for mankind to happen upon their people for as long as their society had been part of the interstellar community. There was a certain kind of fatalism to their attitude, he supposed, like they perhaps felt humans were everything they deserved. They were like lemmings, embracing destruction on a species-wide level, a road to self-annihilation that they probably couldn't explain or even want to get off. Admittedly, some had; the 'bloos living out in the wild were not prepared see their world desecrated or submit to the colonists' dominance, but they were evidently a minority – a rogue genetic strain, maybe, or just the disobedience of youth.

They were, as a race, motivated by guilt, Alpha determined. He stood inside the cramped confines of the museum studying the floridly-written – and badly translated – texts mounted on the walls behind dirty glass frames, which detailed the story of the natives. They themselves had wrought the end of their homeworld, Banar, through an unfortunate by-product of their own evolution: their bodies expelled a gas that the eco-system had struggled to process, and slowly, over the centuries, they'd poisoned their own planet. The atmosphere corroded, vegetation withered, and when it no longer became tenable to live there, they'd sought to relocate to one of its habitable moons. Quite how they'd achieved that remained vague; the documents spoke of them 'seeding' themselves into the stars, but the prosaic reality was more likely that they'd been evacuated by a local relief charity.

The building was cluttered with 'bloo cultural relics and religious iconography. They were a devout species, who worshipped several gods connected with the environment in which they lived – they saw the moon as a divine gift, which had allowed their race to survive, and so it wasn't hard to see why factions were upset at their land's plunder – and had an Original Sin thing going on, which kept them permanently humble and repentant. They were, in the importance they placed on family and fidelity, and the respect they paid to flora and fauna, as considerate a people as you could ever hope to encounter; and, of course, from the unscrupulous companies' point of view, the ideal aliens to have their world stolen out from under them. There were plenty of ore-rich planetoids across the universe that the miners' wouldn't go near because of natives only too keen to make a fight of it, and perhaps on Hegley some of the 'bloos were starting to realise that they didn't have to roll over for the occupiers. There was oblique reference to this change of mood, reading between the lines, as an unspecified revolutionary figurehead was increasingly mentioned.

The museum's curator was human – so little space was afforded to their own racial story that it was too small for a Banabloo to comfortably move around in – and perhaps one of the few colonists sensitive to the aliens' situation. A bustling, passionate middle-aged woman, she was part of the 'hearts and minds' operation that had been flown out to Hegley when Earth first had designs on the moon in a bid to win the residents over and learn more about their ways – the cynical might argue that translated as finding their weaknesses and exploiting them – and had stayed on after the job had been done to carry on researching the 'bloos. She'd been instrumental in helping them build their settlements outside the colony, and the disdain she felt for her fellow Terrans was palpable.

"I'm cataloguing all alien species in this quadrant, as part of my thesis," Alpha told her when he'd finished perusing the artefacts and she'd asked if she could help with anything. He was still dressed in his civvies, shades on, the better to draw the least amount of attention. Fran was back at the motel, administering another painkiller to Wulf. "Banabloos have always interested me."

She nodded enthusiastically, only too happy to talk; obviously she didn't get much in way of visitors. "They are a remarkable people, definitely. Incredibly intelligent, and friendly."

"The thrust of my studies is whether other societies are changing following contact with humans: their relations with one another, their rituals, their temperaments. You know, are we affecting them by our very presence; that kind of thing. Have you seen that with the 'bloos?"

"They've been amazingly accommodating considering what we're doing to their home," she replied, rolling her eyes. "A little *too* soft, some might say. The mining corporations have been dismantling a lot of what's sacred to them, and they're accepting it as part of their gods' plan. There's no question we're changing their landscape around them, but they seem to be as tolerant and forgiving as ever."

"You think that'll last?"

"How do you mean?"

"I understand there are Banabloo elements living out in the wilderness that are militant about the protection of their homeland, and won't kowtow to the humans. I read reports about protest actions against the colony – damage against government buildings, demonstrations, that kind of thing."

"Yes, they're a matter of public record. They're fighting principally for the preservation of their religion – which since it's tied intrinsically to the land is also a fight to safeguard their eco-system."

"Do you think they're going to get worse?"

"They'll get *bolder*, there's no question of that," she answered cautiously. "The further the miners encroach on their terrain, the less the 'bloos will have to lose and the more they'll step up their campaign."

"Are they capable of violence? You said yourself they're a sensitive species."

She looked uncomfortable before replying: "I wouldn't like to say what they could do, bearing in mind their spiritual beliefs are perceived as coming under attack. It goes without saying that I'd hope the galactic authorities would step in before it started to escalate."

"Do you think they'd bomb a shuttle – or at least aid someone who would?"

"You mean, did they cause Flight 307 to crash?" She looked shocked. "God, no. That's way beyond their capabilities. They've never taken a life before; it's unthinkable that they would be involved in something of that magnitude."

"It would enable their cause to hit the headlines."

"No," she said firmly. "The loss of such innocent life is an anathema to them."

"Have you been in contact at all with the militants?"

Her eyes narrowed. "I'm sorry, I don't believe I caught your name. Can you remind me again of your interest in the Banabloos' situation?"

"John Kaye," Alpha replied, proffering a hand, which she pointedly did not shake. The warmth and helpful enthusiasm had drained from her. "Like I said, I'm writing an anthropological thesis, and I'm curious about their psychology. Have you been out into the wastelands, seen what kind of set-up they've got out there?"

"Mr Kaye," she said, "you'll have to excuse my scepticism, but I've been interviewed at great length by the police about my possible sympathies with the 'bloo insurgents. They thought I had contacts with them too. Now, I've made no secret of who I believe is in the wrong with regards to the colonisation of Hegley, but I do not have the natives' ear, nor am I privy to their machinations. Your tone suggests you're following a similar line of questioning to the police, and I'm afraid you're going to be equally disappointed. I am not a fifth columnist, nor am I an honorary member of the Banabloo tribe."

As she was speaking, Johnny had lightly scanned her mind and got a vague impression that she was lying. About what, he couldn't discern in the seconds he had, but she knew more than she was letting on, of that he was certain. But he didn't want to press her too hard, or strong-arm her into releasing information; she was harmless, a good soul with strong convictions.

"I'm sorry if I offended you, that wasn't my intention," he said. "My academic interest sometimes overrides my manners. I didn't mean to insinuate anything."

"If you're that interested in learning more about the 'bloos in the wild, I'd suggest you go out there yourself," she remarked, her body language proclaiming that this was her final word on the subject. "I'll warn you, though – there's a big, empty desert out there and they won't necessarily allow themselves to be found if they don't want to. Human strangers aren't their preferred company."

Sounds like an open invitation, Alpha thought. The longer he was here, the more he believed the truth about Xander Persimmion lay beyond the colony walls.

WULF WAS LOOKING visibly fitter by the time Johnny returned to the motel: up on his feet, pacing the room. He nodded, eyes full of fire, when his partner asked him if he was feeling up for continuing with the case, and threw him his warrant meter.

"Der Doghouse has been back in touch."

Alpha studied it with interest; linked as it was to the Search/ Destroy HQ, information could be swapped between it and agents in the field. They'd confirmed the identity of the gunman, whose mugshot he'd forwarded on to them – he was named as 'Beezle' Bob Flax, a registered Stront. Johnny had never had any dealings with him, though his profile detailed an impressive record as a footsoldier in the Mutant War and he had tallied a not-insubstantial quota of arrests/kills. There was also a cross-reference to half a dozen known associates, all of whom were bounty hunters that again he hadn't encountered but had plenty of past experience and knew their way around a gunfight. Any two of them could've been Flax's co-conspirators on the hit – the Doghouse was not listing active jobs against any of the names, which suggested their whereabouts couldn't necessarily be accounted for. However, it was common for S/D agents to take private jobs off the books – indeed, he and Wulf were here without the GCC's knowledge or approval – so it wasn't always possible to pin down any particular Stront's movements. An agent could be halfway across the galaxy tracking a mark for six months, and no one would be any the wiser as to if or when they'd be returning.

The fact that Flax was on Hegley, attempting to assassinate them, meant someone had contracted him – and most likely other guns-for-hire – on the quiet to both protect the client and prevent the investigation from proceeding. Bodyguarding gigs weren't the usual fare for Stronts, but they weren't unheard of, either; frankly, if the creds on offer were substantial enough, then there wasn't that much that a Dog wouldn't take on. They weren't, on the whole, Alpha had to admit, especially scrupulous when it came to picking and choosing assignments.

"So it *vos* other agents that tried to kill us," Wulf said, catching the meter as Johnny tossed it back.

"Looks like."

"And they knew exactly who ve vere, who they vere planning to take out."

"Without question."

The Viking growled. "By der gotts, is there no honour amongst Dogs like these? Bad enough ve have der criminal voorms gunning for us, but der fellow Stronts too?"

"Never underestimate what some will do for a fat pay cheque."

"Could S/D agents have been paid to bomb the shuttle? They'd have access to the right munitions," Fran said.

"It's possible," Johnny answered, "but I'd like to think that even the most mercenary of Stronts would balk at the murder of innocents – and who was financing them? I can't see the Banabloos scraping together enough capital to convince an agent to blow up a civilian craft, simply to stick it to the colonists." Alpha walked across to where his weapons were hanging over the back of a chair and began strapping on the holsters. "We could do with seeing the manifest, cross-checking who was on board. Could be that one of the passengers was the intended target – a rival ganglord, maybe, or a political opponent. But the cops will have that, and there's no way they'll let us in."

"As far as I'm aware, the police have already followed up on all the victims' backgrounds and no one stood out as a likely target for assassination," the doctor countered. "All of which isn't getting us any closer to finding Xander."

Johnny was about to reply when there was a knock at the door. He opened it to find a surly youth in the motel's uniform, brandishing a small envelope.

"This was left at Reception just now for you, sir."

Alpha nodded his thanks as he took it, tearing it open as he bumped the door shut again with his hip. He swiftly scanned the note.

"Vot is it?"

"It's from the woman I met at the alien historical centre this morning – Jem, she's called, apparently. She says she'd like to see me, has got some info that she'd like to pass on, but wants to do it in public – a cafe in Silver Cross plaza, off the main strip, an hour from now."

"You think it's legit?"

"No way to tell," Alpha said, grabbing his helmet from the nightstand, "but I'm not taking any chances." He glanced at Fran. "You better stay here, doc. Me and the big fella will handle this."

THEY SCOPED IT out thirty minutes before the time they were due to meet her, from a vantage point across the square, but saw nothing untoward – however, they also didn't see the woman enter the premises either. They left it a couple of minutes past the allotted hour, then headed towards the eaterie, threading their way through a crowd that was mainly miners' families out shopping.

The cafe was partially full when they entered, Alpha's eyes roving over the diners, but the woman was not among them.

"She here?" Wulf asked.

"No, can't see her."

"Maybe she get der cold feet."

"We'll give her the benefit of the doubt before we write it off as a bust. Let's take a table and see what happens."

The young waitress was clearly wary of serving a mutant and his strangely accented companion, and kept throwing looks over her shoulder towards her colleagues as if unsure whether the pair should even be allowed to be seated in here. She took their order as perfunctorily as possible and scampered back to the kitchen without looking either of them in the eye. Wulf seethed as he watched her retreating figure, then turned his withering glare on the other patrons until they were discomfited enough to drop their stares.

"Gets kinda tiring, doesn't it?" Johnny commented with a tight smile. "Fighting for your right to be treated like anyone else."

"They don't even disguise it, that's vot angers me. It's like it's der natural thing."

"For many it is. They don't even consider it discrimination, any more than you would feel bad about believing a hog to be beneath you. For them, that's just the way things are, that's the pecking order." Alpha spat the last words out with some vehemence. He was unconsciously fiddling with a napkin as he spoke, tearing it into portions with his fingers.

"I get der sense you've been hardened by it."

"You grow a thick skin, you have to. You isolate yourself. Before, when I was a boy..." His voice trailed off, and he thought better of continuing. "Another time, perhaps."

Their mugs of coffee were brought over and placed down without a word. As the waitress turned to leave, Johnny called her back and explained they were meant to be meeting someone, and asked whether anyone answering to Jem's description – he gave a comprehensive rundown of her features – had passed through the door in the last hour or so. The girl, once coaxed into replying, thought so but admitted that she hadn't seen her leave, either.

"Then vhere?" Wulf said, after the waitress had gratefully returned to the kitchens.

"The bathroom," Johnny replied, nodding at a door on the far wall. He felt uneasy about taking a look in such circumstances – with his ability, he'd learnt early on to respect others' privacy – and tried to limit the penetration of his gaze. He caught sight of a silhouette slumped in one of the cubicles, too awkwardly posed to be natural. "Something's wrong. Wait here."

He crossed over to the toilets and entered with several words of apology to the women washing their hands at the basins. He ignored their protests and knocked on the door of the furthest cubicle; when there was no reply, he shoulder-barged it open. The protests turned into cries for the manager until they saw what he'd found, and then they became shrieks of disbelief. Jem was twisted around on the lavatory, head tipped back, her throat cut wide. Blood had sprayed up the wall behind her. Alpha reached forward and felt for a pulse, knowing it was pointless; she was cold to the touch. He turned and walked out, a roar of horror building behind him. Wulf was already standing, as were many of the diners alerted by the commotion.

"We've got to go," Johnny muttered under his breath. "This place isn't safe."

"Der woman...?"

"Murdered. Somebody was here before us – and probably still is."

The pair exited the cafe, chaos in their wake, and merged into the crowds, just as the first rattle of gunfire split the air, followed by screams. People began to shove each other aside and run. Alpha spun, and saw armed figures at windows all around the plaza taking aim; the first blast had been a warning shot to clear to crush, and now the triggermen had their targets.

The S/D agents had been led into a killzone.

Chapter Seven

For a moment it felt like time had slowed to a crawl. It took Alpha fleeting milliseconds to register the gunmen positioned at the windows, the automatic weaponry that they were sporting, trained on the square below, and realise they were disguised in the same fashion as the hit-team from the other night. His mouth opened to yell a warning to Wulf, but the cry went virtually unheard, drowned out by the roar of five recoilless Newton-Howard blasters opening up simultaneously, breaking the reverie and snapping him back into the here and now. His partner was already moving, the previous day's injury having evidently sharpened his instincts. For a big man, he could shift himself when he needed to, powering forward as shots exploded the rockcrete behind him, ploughing through the rapidly dispersing crowd like the broad prow of a longboat, pushing those in his way down and away from the line of fire. There was little point in Johnny following him, and splitting up would make things more difficult for the shooters, so he threw himself backwards, tumbling through the cafe doorway a moment before a shell took out the plate-glass window frontage and it exploded into countless crystal shards. Screams greeted his arrival, those still left in the building cowering behind upturned tables. The mutant shook off glass fragments and wormed his way to the splintered frame, Westinghouse now gripped in his hand, his eyes searching for Wulf.

He saw him crouched in an alcove, tending to one of the wounded. Many hadn't been fast enough to escape the onslaught; there were a handful of lifeless bodies strewn across the plaza, and twice that of wailing injured. Wulf had ripped a strip of material from the guy's shirt and was trying to tie a make-shift tourniquet to his leg even as blaster fire rained down around them, scorch marks streaking the walls. They couldn't retreat any further, the energy beams criss-crossing ever closer. He finished applying the bandage and with one hand returned fire blindly, spraying in the gunmen's direction, but from where he was hunkered down he couldn't get the elevation. His face was etched with fury and frustration, a lethal anger blossoming in his eyes when he saw one of the unlucky bystanders who was attempting to crawl to safety fried by one of the hit-team's loose blasts.

Johnny had to give him some room. He unhooked a flat disc from his bandolier, and swung it through the window frame, the beam polariser spinning across the square like a Frisbee. Almost instantly the gunfire was drawn away, attracted to the device, following its arc like iron filings trailing after a magnet, and allowing Wulf some respite. The Viking saw his chance and took it. He threw himself out of his hidey-hole, sighted his targets and pumped the trigger, hitting two of the figures in the chest and dropping them to the ground. Alpha stood and did the same, leaving the cover of the café and walking out into the plaza, firing repeatedly, pouring on an equal level of blaster fire to such a degree that the gunmen had to momentarily retreat from the window positions in which they were stationed. But he wasn't going to allow them to regroup.

"Number four cartridge!" A hi-ex shell ripped from the Westinghouse and blew away a section of the facade, brickwork and dust showering those below. "Stay here," he shouted to his partner. "I'll flush them out." He didn't wait for the air to clear and bolted back to the café, demanding the staff tell him how he could reach the second storey. They pointed to a set of stairs leading to a storage area, and he leapt up two steps at a time, slamming between shelves of foodstuffs until he reached the adjoining wall. Barely breaking his run, he carved a hole in it courtesy of a no. 3 round, barrelling into next door's attic space; he'd noted that the properties edging the square were all connected, and constructed to the same flimsy specifications that much of Hegley had been. He took out the next partition with similar ease, putting him directly behind one of the shooters crouching down at his vantage point, rifle cradled in his hands. He caught sight of Alpha, eyes widening in surprise, a second before Johnny drilled a hole in his forehead and the ceiling was sprinkled with crimson flecks.

Burning into the next premises, Johnny found himself standing amidst the destruction that his no. 4 had wrought, a pair of gunmen lying still amidst the wreckage, another sheltering before letting rip with his firearm as he saw Alpha approaching. The S/D agent dodged to one side, the shooter's aim way off, and sent his blaster tumbling out of his hand with a well-aimed shot to the wrist. Johnny closed the distance between them before the guy had time to scrabble for a back-up piece, yanked him to his feet by the scruff of his neck and sent him flailing from the ruined premises onto the plaza below, hitting the rockcrete flagstones with a solid thump. Wulf stepped up and trained his Webley on the groaning figure.

"We need one alive," Alpha called down. "Keep an eye on him. I'm going to try to chase out the rest."

"Johnny – police are coming."

For the first time in the momentary quiet, Johnny heard sirens getting nearer. He glanced at the other windows where the gunmen had been standing, but there was no sign of them; no doubt they had an escape route planned for when the authorities intervened, with or without him and Wulf dead. But their second assassination attempt had failed, and moreover they showed signs of desperation in the collateral damage they were prepared to inflict in a bid to rub out two fellow Stronts. This had been a very public attack; it seemed the orchestrator was spooked.

Johnny clambered down the rubble back to ground level and joined his partner, tugging away the cap and scarf of the prone person at their feet, revealing it to be a woman with short blonde hair, a turquoise cast to her skin and a nose just below her chin, as if it had detached itself and found somewhere on her face more comfortable. He thought he'd seen her round the Doghouse before.

"Who's paying you?" he rasped.

The female mutant smiled thinly and spat into the dust. "Nothin' personal, Alpha. Just a job. But the creds're are too good for me to spill."

"We'll see."

That was all Johnny could glean, however, before all three of them were arrested.

THE AGENTS HAD expected Everson to read them the riot act, but didn't quite anticipate ending up behind bars. They'd come quietly with the cops, not wishing to make their position any more untenable, and hadn't protested when they were stripped of their weapons, but they began to sense that events were spiralling beyond their control when they were frogmarched into a jail cell without further word and left there. There was no clue as to where the woman had been taken.

Johnny had been under police guard before – antagonising the local flatfoots was an occupational hazard for a bounty hunter, and one he'd learnt to deal with calmly and with as little antagonism as possible if he was to ensure a quick and painless release – but being locked up in such a confined space was a new experience for Wulf. He paced the perimeter of the cell like a caged animal, slamming the walls occasionally with his fist, letting loose the odd snarl. He was not a man to be bound without good reason, and Alpha knew better than to try to get a force of nature such as him to sit down and be patient; he wouldn't respond well. Let him ride it out, he thought as he sat on the edge of the bed, watching his partner complete another circuit.

By the time the door rattled open, they'd been left to stew for a couple of hours, the air growing stale and tempers wearing thin. Everson's pompous demeanour as he crossed the threshold made Alpha feel a curl of distaste; he could sense the police chief knew he now had a pertinent reason to hold and possible deport the pair of them, that they'd crossed a line he could at last exploit. That once again they were only defending themselves wouldn't cut any ice, even with one of the hit-team in custody to corroborate their story; he'd warned them against getting into any further shooting matches, and now several Hegley citizens were dead and wounded and a commercial area was half demolished. The chances, Johnny suspected, of them being able to close this case were looking decidedly bleak.

"Well, here we are, mutie," the police chief said, leaning casually with one hand up against the wall. Behind him, a couple of his uniformed cronies lounged in the doorway. "I did say what would happen if you and your trigger-happy pet bear started turning my town into a bullet festival."

"Again, we didn't start anything," Alpha replied wearily. "There's presumably a Stront in a holding cell somewhere that can attest to that."

"Yeah," Everson drawled, unconsciously fingering the cement between the brickwork, "she's not saying much."

"Since when has that stopped good ol' boys in blue like you from extracting a confession?"

"No, I mean she's not saying squat to nobody. She's dead."

Johnny stood, anger radiating from him. He noticed a look of concern pass across Wulf's face, unfamiliar with his friend losing his rag. He'd always been good at bottling his emotions, absorbing every insult, rolling with the incessant and pervasive prejudice. Rarely did the bile rise, but when it did it could be a frightening sight, the cold-blooded air of loathing that he could exude.

"What the hell did you do, Everson?" the S/D agent rumbled.

"Hey, we didn't do nothing... other than maybe my people were a bit lax checking her over when they brought her in. Must've had a pill or something hidden in a tooth, but she was stone-cold in seconds." He snorted. "Can't really blame a man for not wanting to check a freak like that over too closely, you never know what you might find. Or catch. Anyway, saved us a rope; she knew she wasn't going to be going back to mutiehouse central, and took the smart way out."

"This is what passes for law out here, then? Summary execution by hate-mob?"

"It's what we do to terrorists, and we're backed by the GCC to do so." Everson took a step closer to Johnny. "You're getting pretty damn high-minded for a sneckin' bounty hunter, Alpha. Ain't no different to the blood you've spilled in the name of a reward."

"But she vos a living link to whoever vos behind der shuttle bombing," Wulf said. "Der two were connected. Surely you could—"

"Y'know, I've heard all I want to from you, Bjorn. Seem to remember telling you to keep it quiet before."

"So what are you going to do with us?" Johnny asked. "We heading for the long drop too?"

"Alas no, we don't have the authority to pass the death sentence on external agents. But we can keep you locked up here as troublesome elements until the next ship docks and have you dispatched back to wherever you came from."

"Meanwhile, you're no nearer to finding who was behind the Flight 307 explosion."

"Well, the next twenty-four hours should prove pretty decisive," Everson said smugly, turning away from them. "We're moving out into the wastes, turning over those alien dicks that won't play ball. We reckon if we dig deep enough we'll find those responsible."

"Everson, you start messing with the aliens on their own land and you'll have a whole race rising against you. This won't be just protestors anymore; they'll wage war on the colony."

"Guess they should've thought better of harbouring a wanted fugitive, then. Persimmion's out there, hiding amongst the bugs, and we'll finally root him out, see justice done."

"Regardless of vhether he is guilty or not," Wulf commented.

"What did I say," the police chief rasped, spinning back to face the Viking, "about keeping your mouth—"

"Ja, I know: *shut*," the bigger man finished, and landed a punch square in the middle of Everson's face, knocking him to the ground.

The two guards suddenly snapped to attention as they saw their boss go down and piled into the cell, trying to draw their sidearms at the same time, but Johnny was on them in an instant, shoulder-barging them into the wall, driving a knee sharply into the kidneys of one while smacking the other's head off the doorframe. They were unconscious within seconds, Alpha snatching their guns from their holsters, tossing one to his partner.

Everson was sitting upright, one hand held to his bleeding nose. "Sneckin' Stront scum," he croaked through broken cartilage. "I'll have you sneckin' shot—"

"Tie him up with the bedsheet, big fella," Johnny instructed, poking his head out of the door to check the cellblock corridor was empty. Wulf did as he was asked, yanking the police chief to his feet and dumping him onto the bed, hog-tying his wrists and ankles.

"You idiots have just signed your own death warrants," Everson was continuing to rant.

"And shut him up," Alpha added.

The Viking looked around for a moment, his gaze coming to rest on his feet. "Vot vas it you said to Vulf vhen ve first arrived, Everson?" he asked, hopping on to one foot, kicking off his boot and tugging down a thick woollen sock. "Put der sock in it? Maybe you should follow your own advice." He balled up the garment and stuffed in the policeman's mouth as he waggled his head from side to side, emitting muffled grunts, his eyes bulging in outrage.

"Nice improvisation," Alpha commented as his partner slipped his shoe back on.

"Ja, I should patent it. Vot do you think – der... Sternhammer Silencer, maybe?"

"Yeah..." the mutant answered, not sounding convinced. "Pithy. Can't imagine how often you'd need it, though."

They considered trying to find the weapons locker where their equipment would've been stashed, but decided it would delay them too much. Johnny cobbled together enough of a uniform from one of the laid-out guards to make himself look halfway convincing, shut the cell door on the apoplectic Everson, then pushed Wulf ahead as his fake prisoner through the police station. They garnered a few casual glances, but evidently the cops were too busy gearing up for the big assault into Banabloo territory to pay them much heed. Officers clad in body armour and carrying assault rifles trooped past. Without lingering too long, and keeping their heads down, the two of them were out the front entrance and swallowed by the crowds thronging the Hegley streets before the alarm could be raised.

"Ve are getting out of the city, I take it," Wulf said as the two of them kept up a brisk pace.

"No choice now. But it's looking likely that's where our attackers are based, and whomever they're protecting is out there too. If we want to find some answers, we need to head into the wastelands."

"Ve have to go pick up Fran at the motel."

Johnny shook his head. "It's not going to be safe out there for her. You heard what Everson said – they're gonna be cracking down on the 'bloo insurgents, and I'm guessing the natives aren't gonna take it lying down. It'll get nasty, you mark my words."

"It von't be safe for her here, either. Cops vill be hunting for us, vill track down vhere ve are staying, and find her. I vould feel better knowing she vas with us."

"I can't guarantee her safety. Look at us: we've got nothing but these police-issue pop-guns. We're in no position to be going into a firefight, much less bringing a civilian along as well. She'll be a liability."

The Viking stopped and brought his partner to a halt too, his face grave. "If her husband is out there, she should be der first to know. She came all der way from Earth 'cause she couldn't rest not knowing vhere he vas – she deserves to see him."

"He could be a murderer, for all she knows. He might be dead."

"Then she should find that out for herself."

"Look, big guy, you're as compassionate and honourable a norm as I've ever met, but you gotta remember she's still the client. You can't lose sight of that, you can't let it cloud your judgement."

"And ve should not forget vot it is ve are doing here, der reason ve took der job. She came to us for help – ve can't shut her out vhen it means so much to her."

Alpha studied his friend for a moment. "You're a softy at heart, aren't you?"

"I... vould like to bring her peace of mind."

Johnny held up his hands. "Okay, okay, we'll go fetch her. But she's your responsibility, right? You're in charge of keeping her alive."

"Ja, no problem. Talking of which, I left der Happy Stick in the motel room. I must take that with me."

"Believe me, from now on, Wulf, I wouldn't let it leave your hand..."

Chapter Eight

THEY STOPPED AT a down-at-heel skimmer rental outlet that didn't ask too many questions and was willing to lease them a pair of dubiously safe rustbuckets for a nominal fee. Clearly the guy behind the counter didn't have much confidence he'd be getting the vehicles back, casting a wary eye over the strange threesome, but figured that the insurance was worth more than the bikes themselves. He was also beholden to mention, perhaps picking up a fugitive vibe, that the cops were mobilising out beyond the colony, that citizens were being advised to stay within its walls. Alpha thanked him and didn't attempt to spin a yarn about where they were going: the man knew they were evading the law but would say nothing, for fear of incurring an investigation into his own practices. The mutant kicked his ride into life and peeled off towards one of Hegley's exits, Wulf piloting the second skimmer behind him with Fran perched on the pillion, hands gripping his sides.

She'd needed little encouragement to come with them, Alpha mused as he guided the vehicle past the police checkpoint on the edge of colony territory. He accelerated when a uniform tried to flag him down, leaving him choking on his dust. When the S/D agents had intimated that they believed answers lay out in the Banabloo hinterlands, she'd immediately insisted on joining them, desperation writ large on her face. Johnny had noted a softness in her gaze as she'd smiled hopefully at Wulf and sensed a connection between the two, a touch of loneliness bonding them. Her life had been paralysed by loss and a lack of closure; he was a man out of time, a stranger in a strange future, still coming to terms with the world in which he found himself, despite his bravado. A pair at odds with their surroundings, they evidently saw a kinship in each other which they both gained from.

Zipping over the terrain, they could see the stark outlines of the mining works on the horizon, great steel skeletons looming against the sky. The machinery worked night and day, drilling and scouring for the mineral ore that was the fuel base for most interstellar flight, and even from this distance you were aware of the incessant grind, the ground trembling beneath your touch if you put a hand to it. Johnny had heard that the rock-jockeys working their shifts at the remote stations were virtually outlaws, revelling in the lack of constraints or authority, the companies letting them run pretty much autonomously. They were prone to go a little crazy too, embracing the frontier spirit a mite too enthusiastically – far from the barely civilising influence of Hegley, and many light-years from home, they went as wild as the landscape, reliving the cowboy experience of their forebears. Alpha didn't want to tussle with them if he could help it, and widely skirted any mining operations still active on their route, the rumbling of the gears and hiss of hydraulics fortunately masking their journey. He could just about discern that they'd caught the curious attention of figures climbing derricks or guards positioned on watchtowers, binox focusing in their direction, but no one hailed them or questioned their presence.

Deeper into the wastelands they headed, the landscape as pitted and inhospitable as they'd been led to believe, mostly barren rock punctuated by Banabloo mounds. The aliens seemed to live in clusters – villages, Johnny surmised – a ring of a dozen or so nests often centred on what looked like totem poles. There appeared no rhyme or reason as to where the 'bloo settlements were built; there was no discernible difference between one stretch of ground and the next. The monotonous grey-brown earth unrolled before them with little evidence of vegetation or water. Hegley really was an unattractive mudball.

Some of the camps looked abandoned, with no sign of life; in others Alpha saw glittering eyes watching them go past, a hint of movement behind soil walls. They were unnervingly reluctant to poke their heads out of their homes, just a curling black mass shifting in the shadows, which was somehow more intimidating than if they'd scuttled across their path and had them surrounded. Johnny was left with the sense that they were seething behind the scenes, beneath the rock at his feet or in the canyons and valleys they passed through, veiled from sight but close enough to strike. His skin prickled at the thought, and he wondered if the authorities were aware of what a potentially formidable foe they were intent on antagonising.

Wulf pulled up alongside him as they scooted down an incline. "Dey are not der most welcoming of creatures in their own habitat," he remarked.

"If your land was being strip-mined from under you, you might be more than a bit wary of humans."

The Viking looked around disparagingly at the dull expanse. "Dey are welcome to it. It is hardly paradise."

"Each to their own." Alpha shrugged. "It might not be much, but it's theirs."

"But these timid creatures are der militants der police want to crack down on?"

"No, the cops will be targeting known insurgents nearer the colony. They'll be convinced that Xander and his band of rebels are operating on the outskirts."

"Then where are we heading?" Fran shouted over the engine roar.

"Wulf and I saw a map back at the 'bloo township – there was an area that your husband may well have been interested in hiding out in right from the start. It was kind of vague, hard to pinpoint, but something I noticed earlier allowed me to narrow where to look. Remember the female Stront, the one the police pulled in and who died during her interrogation?"

"Vot about her?"

"She had a slight blue pigmentation to her skin. The norms probably dismissed that as part of her mutation, but I'd seen her around the Doghouse before; she didn't have it then. It's a byproduct of being in a certain spot – miners get it when they're exposed to gases. She could only have picked it up in one particular corner of the moon."

"You know where that is?" the doctor asked.

"I've an idea," Alpha replied. "Follow me."

They sped on.

THEY CRESTED A ridge after a further twenty minutes' hard ride, and Johnny motioned for them to stop. Fran started to say something, but Wulf shifted around on the skimmer and put a finger to his lips, nodding at his partner. The mutant was scanning the landscape below, squinting in concentration; a moment later, he swung his leg off the bike and beckoned them over, urging them stay crouched and quiet.

"Vot can you see?" Wulf whispered.

"Camouflaged camp down in the valley," Alpha answered. "Very well disguised; probably would've passed right by it if I didn't have the eyes." He looked back over his shoulder. "There's the lip of a crater that hides it from view on the north and east sides. That might be why Xander was so interested in this area on the map, that it made such a good natural hiding place. Could see a handful of bodies on the ground, not too many."

"Stronts?"

"Couldn't tell from this distance, but we'll have to assume they are." Johnny shuffled to look first at the Viking, then at Fran. "Wulf, you follow my lead; we're short on weapons, so we'll have to take them out as stealthily as we can. Doctor, I think it's best you stay here out of harm's way. We'll let you know once it's safe to enter."

"Take this," Wulf said, offering her his police-issue blaster. "You vill need some protection if you are discovered."

"I've never fired anything in my life—" she started, turning the weapon over in her hands.

"Better you have it und don't need it," he countered, showing her where the safety release was. "Point, pull trigger, der gun does der rest. I found it easy to master."

"But what about you?"

"I have der Happy Stick. I can improvise."

She nodded, and watched as the two agents carefully descended the bank, scooting down through the shale to the valley floor. Once shielded by an outcropping, Alpha gave the set-up another once-over, then indicated a sparsely guarded entrance where a figure was lounging. He was a mutant, all right, and wearing an S/D badge. Johnny closed his eyes and furrowed his brow.

"Vot now?"

"Just planting a little curiosity in his mind..."

Wulf peered over the top of the boulder and saw the guard suddenly jump to his feet and anxiously glance around, swinging his gun to bear at every shadow, all the time drifting nearer to the two agents. He waited until the guard had moved past him before stepping out behind him and clonking him on the head with his warhammer; the guard crumpled without a sound.

"Neat trick," he said as he palmed the unconscious mutant's blaster. "I didn't know you could do that."

"Doesn't always work," Alpha admitted. "Depends on the gullibility of the subject. It's kind of like going into someone's house and moving their furniture around without them noticing. Took a bit of chance, but I should've guessed that the Stronts working this gig wouldn't be big on smarts."

They edged through the entrance into the camp – it resembled a paramilitary compound, with a handful of rudimentary bunks to their right and a cookhouse beyond. There were several tents scattered beneath the camouflage covering; another mutant perched on a stool outside the largest, cleaning his gun. Johnny gave it the eye, nodded at his partner, and pointed a route to come at the tent from the rear. They scurried carefully between the canvas structures until they rounded on the seated figure. Alpha put his gun to the guy's temple.

"Not a sound," he murmured, kicking to one side the mutant's partly disassembled rifle. "Xander Persimmion's in there, right?"

A nod.

"Okay, you're going to be our leverage. On your feet."

He yanked the guard up with one hand, blaster barrel still planted to his head, and shoved him into the tent. Inside were stacks of documents and a laptop set up on trestle table; in the foreground, a handsome middle-aged norm on crutches was standing between three Stronts, engaged in a heated exchange, which ended abruptly as the newcomers entered, and for a second they simply stared. Then the weapons were drawn.

"Dr Persimmion, I presume?" Johnny said.

"Alpha? What are you...? I thought the cops had you in custody."

"Yeah, well, sorry to disappoint. You can't keep a good Dog down. However, this kind of Dog" – he jammed the gun harder against his captive's head – "I could put down without any great hardship at all. So why don't your friends there drop the hardware and walk away?"

"They're going nowhere. You should never have come here, Alpha – you and your pal, you should never have taken this job, never gone near Hegley. I can't let you leave, not now."

"What's the deal here, doc? You got half the moon looking for you, and you're holed up like a terrorist with hired bodyguards. You really plant the bomb on that shuttle?"

"I'm saying nothing. You don't understand, you two are in way over your heads—"

"But your vife is desperate to find you," Wulf interrupted, taking a step forward. "She came here looking for answers."

"My *wife*?" The colour drained from Persimmion's face. "You're... you're telling me she's on Hegley right now?"

"Ja. She vanted to know you were still alive—"

Gunfire ripped through the tent: three successive bursts that took out the doctor's guards. Johnny spun, letting go of the mutant, and in that instant another round dropped him too. Fran emerged, smoking blaster held in both hands, and cast a cursory eye over the four dead bodies to make sure they were dead. Then she smiled at Alpha and Wulf before turning her attention to her husband, gun raised.

"Xander... you don't know how long I've waited for this moment."

Chapter Nine

"WHAT... WHAT THE sneck is this?" Persimmion stammered.

"Oh, Xander, I always *knew* you were still alive," Fran said, smiling. "There was a part of me that always believed – when we heard that your body hadn't been recovered from the shuttle wreckage – that you'd escaped, that you were somewhere on Hegley. I just had to make sure – and here you are, honeybun, large as life."

"Okay, doc, what's going on here?" Johnny demanded, fixing his attention on the woman. "What kind of game are you playing? You told us you'd never fired a gun before—"

"Yeah, that wasn't strictly true. Just part of the act."

"Act?" Wulf rumbled. "You have been lying to us? This *is* your husband?"

"That's not Fran," Persimmion said quietly, backing away slightly. "They've sent—"

"Okay, okay, that was another untruth," the woman admitted, holding her hands up in mock contrition. "A major embellishment on my part. But I figured there was a better chance of hiring two bounty dogs to find the missing Xander Persimmion if they were faced with the grieving widow and parent. Why do the hard graft when you can have someone else take out the opposition for you?"

"Sir, we heard gunfire," a voice called, a moment before the tent flap was pulled back revealing a further two Stronts. The woman instantly raised her weapon and snapped off two headshots, blowing them backwards, blood misting the air. She caught Alpha's eye, read his intention, and shot his right wrist, forcing him to drop his own gun; he yelled, clutching at the injury. In the same movement, she kicked Wulf's gun from his grasp; the Viking was already swinging his warhammer in retaliation when she ducked low and lashed out at his knee with her heel, bringing him crashing to the ground with a grunt. The entire action had taken less than three seconds, one fluid, professional strike in which it looked like her pulse was barely raised. She stepped over to the whimpering doctor and forced him to his knees, one hand clutching his shirt collar, the other pushing the gun barrel to the back of his head.

"Quite the little army you've got at your disposal, Xander," she said. "Any more I should be aware of?"

He shook his head.

"That it?" she persisted, pushing him down further.

He nodded quickly.

"Kind of ironic, you surrounding yourself with muties, don't you think? What was the reasoning behind it – cannon fodder, or an acknowledgement that they're actually pretty good in a fight?"

"Cheap, plentiful," he muttered, "and they don't ask questions."

"Ha! No argument there. A woman with a sob story can walk into the Doghouse and claim to be anyone. If the money's right, who amongst that bunch of vultures is going to challenge you?" She met Alpha's burning gaze. One hand was holding his wounded lower arm, stemming the blood flow, but he was edging forward. The gun immediately left the back of Persimmion's head and was pointed in the S/D agent's direction. "Stay where you are, John. You know I can use this."

"So who are you?" Alpha snarled. "Did Fran Persimmion even exist?"

"Oh, she existed. Isn't that right, doc?" She lightly batted Persimmion's head with the gun. He whimpered in agreement. "Wife to Xander, mother to poor little Iris... and also a high-ranking member of the Purity League."

"Der who?"

"Mutant haters," Alpha said, his eyes not leaving the woman. "Norm extremists. Genetic fascists."

"Some on the fringes of our group are a touch... enthusiastic," she said airily, "but it's a legitimate party, and one with considerable support within the establishment. If mankind is to survive, bloodline is sacred; the mutant gene has to be weeded out. We're just facing a future of birth defects and a tainted species otherwise." She glanced fondly at the man prone at her feet. "The Persimmions were very good at research on that front."

"You vere both involved?" Wulf asked the doctor.

"Quite the power couple," the woman answered. "With their status and connections, they had access to some of the best pharmaceutical equipment and technology. Their role, at least on the surface, was tackling and arresting infant mortality amongst the mutants; what it gave them was the inside track to developing a set of boosters and immunisation jabs that would slowly decimate a particular section of the population over time, targeted for those with rogue DNA. Shortened lifespans, increased susceptibility to viral infection... we'd see the mutant problem dealt with over the course of a couple of generations. Nothing outright nasty, just giving the freaks a helpful shove out of the way so decent humans can get on with the business of evolving."

"You've administered these injections?" Johnny said, barely able to contain his fury.

"No, not yet. You want to know why? Because this spineless buffoon" – she kicked Persimmion sharply in the midriff, and he rolled groaning onto his side – "chickened out. Ten years of work and he had a change of heart, destroyed a lot of the samples. It was probably having the sprog that did it; it can make even the most ardent believers go gooey-eyed useless. He didn't tell the PL he was no longer on board, of course; he was still trying to work out a way to get out in one piece. But Fran began to suspect that he was sabotaging the tests... and then he became aware that she was on to him. We anticipated he was going to make a run for it."

"Der flight to Hegley..."

"Another annual medical conference on the mining colony, nothing unusual about that; but we guessed he was going to hop on an outgoing shuttle with his daughter once there, and disappear. We couldn't risk him going public – he was a liability that could compromise the entire League. Fran accepted that he had to be silenced. She knew where her loyalties lay."

"But her child—"

"Like I say, she'd made her peace with it."

"But he escaped," Alpha said, wincing, his arm growing numb. "In fact, he'd been planning his escape for at least a year beforehand. He'd been talking to the Banabloos about a place he could hide."

"Yeah, and that's the part I've been dying to hear," the woman declared, turning back to Persimmion, who had curled into a ball. "I couldn't in all good conscience whack you, doc, without first hearing how you came out of the crash intact."

"Doesn't matter," he whispered. "You're going to kill me anyway."

"Nah, that's not playing fair. Can't leave us dangling. How about this for an incentive?" She stamped suddenly on the thumb of his left hand, the crack of bone sounding like a gunshot. He howled, tears streaming down his cheeks. "I won't break the other nine if you 'fess up right now."

"Time bomb... limited field," he breathed. "Miniature device; I had the displacement core hidden behind the lens of my glasses, which got it past the spaceport scanners. Rest was homemade, in pieces in my hand luggage, ready to be assembled."

"You *knew* there was an explosive device on the shuttle," Alpha said. "That's why you came pre-armed."

He nodded shakily. "I overheard Fran talking on the phone, intercepted some messages, and realised they were going to plant a bomb on the ship—"

"The chief executive of the airline is... sympathetic to the League's cause," the woman interjected. "Got a lackey to wire up the explosive while the shuttle was on the runway in New London."

"I had to go through with the Hegley trip, or they would have come after me; I had to make it look like I'd perished with the rest of the passengers. My work in the mutant ghettoes had brought me into contact with several Stronts – they thought I was doing good work. When I explained that I needed to disappear, they helped me come up with a solution."

"They didn't ask why you had to vanish?"

"Stronty Dogs aren't big on asking questions if there are creds on the table. They gave me the guts of a time bomb, and I hired them to provide the support. The plan was that once we were in the moon's atmosphere and the displacer was activated, it would generate a field to take both Iris and me back in time for thirty or so seconds, by which point the shuttle would've moved on. If I'd got my maths right, we would've materialised in the Stronts' ship that was going to be following the same flight path. Then we would've got the hell out of Dodge."

"Vot went wrong?"

"Everything, pretty much. Couldn't get the time bomb to work properly; it didn't widen the field enough to accommodate..." – he swallowed, eyes leaking – "to accommodate Iris as well as me, and when it went off I'd missed the slot. I fell a fair few feet, bashed myself up quite badly." He gestured to the crutches lying beside him. "It was then that I discovered I was alone, that Iris... hadn't made it."

"Huh," the woman muttered. "Quite the scheme."

"The Stronts found me and we hid out in a spot I'd earmarked while they patched me up. In the wake of the shuttle crash, the Hegley authorities had the colony on lockdown, weren't allowing any craft to leave without authorisation. I thought I'd lay low until the coast was clear – or as long as I still had the funds to pay my bodyguards. But then I heard that people were looking for me, that other S/D agents were on-planet and sniffing around." He looked pitifully at Johnny and Wulf. "I *had* to try to stop you; I had to protect myself. I'm sorry."

"Too late for guilt now, Xander dearest," she smirked.

"Too late? I haven't *stopped* feeling guilty; I haven't slept since the shuttle went down. When I think of the innocent lives lost – of my own daughter – I wish I'd just taken my chances with the Purity League."

"But you didn't, did you? You ran, and dragged your own kid into it. Face it, you're a pathetic coward as well as spineless."

"You still haven't told us who *you* are," Alpha said to the woman.

"Me? My name is unimportant. I'm simply a cleaner for the PL, a troubleshooter, extremely well trained in shielding their thoughts from prying eyes." She winked at him. "I knew you'd try it at least once, Johnny-boy. Anyway, when my superiors heard that Xander's body hadn't been found, they went batshit – ordered me to tidy up the loose ends. I stopped by the Persimmion home and duly silenced Fran. If I was to find the missing husband, I thought I'd adopt the identity of a desperate wife, anxious to know that he was all right, and to be reunited."

"The coroner… Dendry. He thought there was something different about you when we met him at the morgue."

"I had some minor surgery to model my appearance closer to Fran's. Familiarised myself with her work too. I had to be convincing if I was going to persuade someone to help me."

"When in fact you just wanted to make doubly sure Xander was dead," Johnny said.

"Hey, if a job's worth doing," she replied and put the handgun to Persimmion's head and pulled the trigger, blasting away half his cranium. He slumped face down. She walked towards the agents. "I hope you don't take this personally, John. Or you, Wulf. I picked you 'cause I heard you were good, but if you hadn't taken the assignment, then those two other idiots from the Doghouse could've been here in your place. I doubt they would've survived to this point, but still: it was just chance that our paths crossed and I ended your lives. No hard feelings. You got a tough break."

"All this way, all this charade, to make sure one man was dead…" Alpha said, his gaze fixed on hers.

"That's correct. Call it closure." She aimed her gun at him.

"… and you couldn't even get *that* right. Guy's still alive. Point blank and you still missed him."

Doubt furrowed her brow, and the gun wavered. "What are talking about? I just blew his head off."

"No, you're mistaken. He's still breathing. Check him yourself."

"I killed him, I'm sure I…"

"Look." Johnny's pupil-less eyes gleamed.

"Shut up, I don't need to…"

"But you can't be sure, can you?" He felt the alpha waves washing through her skull, nudging her thought processes, erasing certainty, just ever so slightly tipping her towards confusion. There was a lot of resistance, but he only needed to plant the tiniest doubt…

"Dammit—" She cast an eye over her shoulder, the blaster dropping a fraction.

Johnny took his chance and threw himself forward, colliding with the woman while she was distracted. She yelped and staggered, the gun barking and drilling a slug into the ground. He fixed his good hand around her wrist and yanked it, trying to force her to release the weapon, but she had a strong grip and wouldn't relinquish it. She aimed a punch with her free fist and pounded on his wounded arm, shockwaves reverberating through his body. He slackened his hold on her and she tore free.

"Goddamn piece of shit mutant," she muttered, swinging the gun up once more into Johnny's face, but in that moment a warhammer came flying between them and smashed it out of her hand. She screamed, clutching at her fingers, and backed away as Wulf approached, anger etched on his features. He reached out for her but she was quicker, dodging under his arms and shoulder-charging into his solar plexus, driving the air from his lungs. Her momentum carried them both back and he toppled, while she rolled and sprang to her feet. She dashed for the tent flap.

Alpha scrambled for a gun amongst the dead Stronts, found one, and came up blasting. But his gun-hand was barely functioning, numbness stealing into his digits. The shots went wild as the weapon trembled, and she scooted out of the tent unharmed.

Wulf clambered upright and retrieved his Happy Stick. "She vill be making for der skimmers."

"Don't think I could ride one," Johnny said. "Arm's screwed; got no strength in it. Can't shoot, either."

"You stay here, then. I vill go after her."

"Be careful. She's banking on us following her, waiting for a chance to take a shot. She'll be out for blood." He threw his partner his purloined gun.

Wulf caught it, already striding through the entrance, turning to look back at Johnny with murderous intent in his eyes. "I vill not disappoint her."

Chapter Ten

Wulf was no more than three feet from the encampment when the first shot rang out. He felt the air part, heard the boulder to his left crack and splinter a few inches from his head, and he was racing for cover before the second bullet found its target. He weaved towards the bottom of the ridge, breathing hard, knowing that if he hesitated for even a moment in the open she would put him in the dirt. Further bullets pockmarked his zigzag path. As he ran, he tried to glance up to gauge her position, but all he could see was unforgiving dull rock spread before him and a million places a shooter could choose to hide.

He paused to snatch some air beneath a promontory and for a brief few seconds flashbacked to his life in Norstad, before he met Johnny, before his life took its sudden deviation away from all that he knew. He'd joined raiding parties plenty of times in his old guise, terrorising the coastal villages of the Anglo-Saxons and the Franks, plundering wealth and livestock, enslaving those that didn't fall to their swords, and he and his fellow warriors had faced similarly hostile terrain as they'd come charging off their longboats, any number of surprises awaiting them around each corner. Their success despite the odds, despite entering unknown territory, he always put down to their utter conviction, a belief in their own imperviousness, that no well-aimed arrow or lucky axe strike could dent. They were immortal, forged in iron, fire in their blood, born for battle; they could not be stopped any more than the tide.

He thought of those moments just before they hit land, blade slick in his hand, shield heavy on his arm, hammer slung across his back, when the heart pumped furiously and his muscles tensed, his frame coiled for attack. Injury or death did not concern him; he did not anticipate them. Such fates awaited lesser mortals, those not protected by the watchful eye of Odin; it was *they* who would tremble at his coming, who would feed the wolf. The adrenaline surge that had powered through him then as he'd steeled himself for the assault he could feel returning to him now, emboldening him – he'd faced down far greater challenges than a single enemy. Though she may try to take him out, he would pass through her attempts unscathed, because he was the stronger, the Sternhammer, and all buckled beneath his shadow.

With a roar, he charged, ascending the incline at speed, and in that instant he saw her, standing from cover, fixing him in her sights. He did not break his stride as he raised his own weapon and pumped the trigger, dimly aware of her shot notching the meat of his bicep, but he was no longer able to stop even if he wanted to; the berserker fury was upon him and such superficial injuries would not quell it. She dashed for shelter but he poured on the gunfire and caught her in the leg and shoulder, spinning her onto her back, her gun flying from her. He reached her before she could crawl away; her eyes showed fear for the first time as he loomed over her, blaster pointed at her head, a terrifying vision of a beast unleashed.

"Let's... let's talk about this," she hissed, wincing as she scrabbled backwards.

"There is nothing to say," he rumbled, his voice seemingly coming from deep within his chest, dark and menacing; the reiver he once was returned.

"I can pay. You're a... a merc, a bounty hunter. There's always a price, right? I can make it... worth your while."

"Your money has no value, old cucumber," he replied, standing on her left arm to prevent her moving any further. "Your life has no value. There is nothing you can offer me to take you alive. You und all der scum you represent."

"S-screw you then," she muttered and lashed out with her right hand; he hadn't seen her pull the blade from her belt. The knife punctured his inner thigh as she drove it in as far as she could; he barked in pain, legs crumbling, releasing her from where she was pinned. She pulled herself to her feet and staggered towards the top of the ridge, dragging her wounded limb behind her. Wulf gritted his teeth and tugged the dagger free, blood flooding in its wake, and he fought to hold back the nausea that welled up alongside it. He heard the sound of a skimmer engine being kickstarted into life and limped quickly after it.

As he crested the ridge he saw her tearing away, heading back towards the colony. He threw himself onto the saddle of the remaining bike, twisted the throttle, and tried to keep it stable as it lurched after her, the vehicle pounding against his aching body. Her skimmer was veering wildly; it looked like she was also struggling to control it. She was possibly lapsing in and out of consciousness, the gunshot injuries taking their toll.

Wulf sighted his blaster as best he could, following her erratic course with the gun barrel, and took a shot – the first ploughed a hole in the earth as she swerved violently, the second punched through the bike's engine, pitching it forward. Amazingly, it remained upright, but black smoke was billowing from beneath the chassis and it was losing power as he found himself catching up with her. He realised that they were heading towards one of the Banabloo villages that they'd previously passed and, even though her bike was coughing a horrible, throaty death rattle that signalled it wasn't long for this world, she was still going at some speed. He could see her yanking on the handlebars, but the skimmer wouldn't turn.

He tried to push forward and get alongside the woman, see if he could nudge her out of the way of the structures. The front of his vehicle clipped the rear of hers just as they reached the settlement's outskirts, and her skimmer jack-knifed and skidded at ninety degrees into the base of the nearest 'bloo nest with a shuddering crunch. She threw herself from it, wheezing from smoke inhalation, flames licking at the bike's engine. Part of the alien mound collapsed under the impact, tumbling onto the wreckage, and black shapes roiled inside.

By the time Wulf had brought his skimmer to a halt and got off, the woman had half crawled, half staggered to the totem at the centre and was leaning against it for support. She saw him approaching, looked back at the sculpture next to her, grabbed hold of a lower extremity and yanked it free. On closer inspection, he discovered that the totem pole consisted of artfully composed bones, though their origin – Terran, Banabloo or otherwise – wasn't immediately obvious; what the woman was currently brandishing looked disturbingly like a sharpened femur. He pointed his gun, too weary from blood loss to speak, aware that the native creatures were starting to swarm around them.

"What you doing here?" a voice chittered as one of the 'bloos broke from the ranks and scuttled between the two humans, rising on its hind legs. "No place for humans here!"

"Get lost, freak," the woman answered, her breathing shallow, her gore- and soot-streaked face slack, attention fixed on Wulf.

"No place here!" the alien repeated, its tone rising, its antennae twitching. "Go now!" The Viking had never seen them looking as distressed as this, as angry; red flecks flared in the 'bloo's eyes. These weren't natives used to dealing with the colonists – they took trespassing very seriously. Wulf dropped his blaster and held out his hands in a placatory gesture, not wishing to aggravate them further; the humans were in a precarious position here. The woman, however, had other ideas.

"Stay the hell away from me," she rasped, swinging the shard of bone in the alien's direction, swaying slightly. It backed up, hissing, the other creatures echoing its displeasure and swirling closer. She seemed not to notice the danger, looking ever more demented. "I said, stay back, sneckin' filth!" She jabbed her makeshift weapon and carved a bloody gouge from the 'bloo's hide, the alien letting loose a hideous screech.

It stunned them all into silence. For a brief moment, realisation crossed her features as she saw the situation she was in. Her mouth dropped open in panic, her eyes locking with Wulf's. Then the swarm was on her, and she disappeared under a black seething mass. The darkness too closed over the S/D agent; he was pushed to the ground, forced to curl up into a ball, arms wrapped around his head to protect it from the many tramping feet, while the screaming echoed around him.

WHEN WULF OPENED his eyes again, he was still surrounded by noise, though what had been a keening, high-pitched cry was now a more distant dull *thud* interspersed with shouted orders. It took him a second of consciousness to recognise small-arms fire. He sat up sharply, then felt a hand on his shoulder gently persuading him not to rise any further.

"Take it easy, pal," Johnny said, appearing from behind him. His right arm was in a sling. "We're okay."

"Vhere...?"

"We're in the 'bloo reservation attached to the colony. I made it to the nearest mining outpost and convinced them to give me a ride back. You were brought here by the aliens, so I'm told; it looks like they patched you up."

The Viking looked down at himself, aware for the first time that he was lying on a blanket in a 'bloo construct. His leg was bandaged with a papery substance, but it felt secure and comfortable. Behind Johnny squatting next to him, he could see a few curious eyes glinting through the doorway. "Der woman?"

Alpha shook his head. "No sign. Can you remember anything?"

The image of her vanishing beneath those coiling black forms remained imprinted on his mind; then he thought of their totem, that column of bones. "She's gone."

"Dead?"

Wulf nodded. Johnny could see that he was holding something back, something that he didn't want to vocalise, so didn't push him. The poor guy was still getting used to what this galaxy could throw at them. There was another faint crack of gunfire and his partner looked questioningly at him.

"Police are still engaged in fighting with the 'bloo insurgents. I think they've underestimated them; by all accounts it's not going well for the colonists."

"Ja, that I can believe."

"We're also still *persona non grata* here – cops are going to be looking for us. The 'bloos are happy for us to stay until we can get off-planet. I've contacted Middenface at the Doghouse and he's sorting transportation to pull us out. It could get hairy if the authorities catch wind of a ship sneaking into their airspace, but hopefully they've got enough on their plate at the moment."

"How long?"

"Another day, perhaps."

Wulf was silent for a moment, then said: "I'm sorry, Johnny. It vos my fault ve ended up in this mess."

"Don't be ridiculous. You couldn't have known."

"You said not to trust a norm, that ve should not get involved."

"She played us both, and if it hadn't have been us, then some other poor sap would've taken a bullet to the back of the head. Anyway, she wasn't a typical norm; she was... something else."

"Der Purity League."

"Yeah, we've got unfinished business with them once we get off this rock. If they're still aiming to roll out their fake immunisation programme, we need to put a spoke in their plan."

The Viking ran a hand through his beard and sighed. "I keep thinking of der innocents that needlessly died, der Persimmion girl... sacrificed. Der sheer ruthlessness of it."

Johnny stood and gave his partner a reassuring pat on the arm. "Nothing changes, does it, big fella?" He walked towards the doorway, the eavesdropping Banabloos scampering away at his approach. "Nothing ever changes."

ABOUT THE AUTHOR

Matthew Smith was employed as a desk editor for
Pan Macmillan book publishers for three years before joining
2000 AD as assistant editor in July 2000 to work on a comic he
had read religiously since 1985. He became editor of the Galaxy's
Greatest in December 2001, and then editor-in-chief of the 2000
AD titles in January 2006. He lives in Oxford.

FIND US ONLINE!

www.rebellionpublishing.com

/rebellionpub   /rebellionpublishing   /rebellionpub

SIGN UP TO OUR NEWSLETTER!

rebellionpublishing.com/sign-up

YOUR REVIEWS MATTER!

Enjoy this book? Got something to say?

Leave a review on Amazon, GoodReads or with your favourite bookseller and let the world know!

Made in United States
Troutdale, OR
05/22/2025

31596505R10059